THE Y SYNDROME

and good luck to women who help women.

*Ruth
March, 2021*

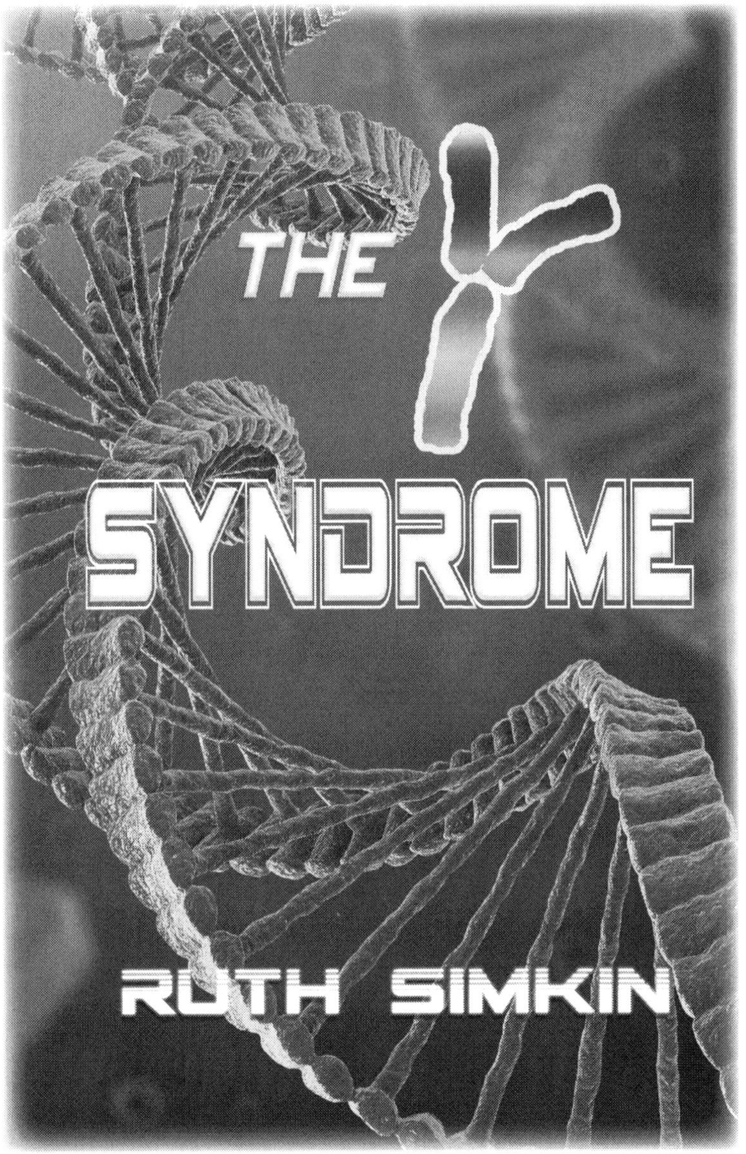

THE Y SYNDROME

RUTH SIMKIN

Bink Books
Bedazzled Ink Publishing Company • Fairfield, California

© 2017 Ruth Simkin

All rights reserved. No part of this publication may be reproduced or transmitted in any means, electronic or mechanical, without permission in writing from the publisher.

978-1-945805-57-8 paperback

Cover Design
by

Bink Books
a division of
Bedazzled Ink Publishing, LLC
Fairfield, California
http://www.bedazzledink.com

ACKNOWLEDGEMENTS

Books don't exist on their own. Even though the author is credited with writing the book, many people have input and help realize thoughts and words onto pages. Thank you to all of my friends and family who have supported me and helped me; there are so many. I can't name all of you, but I do thank you all. In particular, thank you to:

Dvora Levin, my literary compatriot, who has my utmost gratitude for being my "first reader." I can't imagine writing a book without her valued involvement;

Rodney Muir, my Calgary Cohort, from whom I received much helpful information and encouragement. I am also grateful for her friendship of almost half a century;

Chris Wilson, my computer genius who keeps my home running smoothly and incredibly competently with all things electronic and keeps me running by being one of my most cherished friends; Estelle Kurier, Sheila Hatswell, Marvin Kurier, and Angie Peppar for keeping my home and me running smoothly while I write;

Kelly, who makes me laugh every day;

My family, including sibs Judi Simkin, Jack and Nanci Simkin, Sam and Carol Simkin and all my multitudinous relatives, especially Maddy Santner, for being so supportive of my writing;

C.A. Casey and Claudia Wilde from Bedazzled. When a writer first works with a new publisher, she is never sure about what she will get. Claudia and Casey have been two very helpful and extremely competent publishers and editors as well as being lots of fun to work with, something which is very important to me. I thank them and Bedazzled for everything they have done to produce this book.

SEPTEMBER 18, 1992

PATTY PUSHED HER way through the crowd, trying to get to the top of the stairs. She paused for a minute to look around, her heart beating faster in anticipation of the March. A feeling of excitement tinged with fear infiltrated the crisp September air as the women began to gather. Hundreds of women converged in the plaza and on the steps leading up to city hall look around, Patty stood on tiptoe, looking over a multitude of heads, seeing police gather off to one side behind the large banner, blood red, which proclaimed "Women Take Back The Night."

As Patty ascended the stairs, her blonde ponytail got caught in another banner as it was being unfurled. She disentangled herself, took a step backwards to look at the black banner with white writing blaring out: "Dead Men Don't Rape."

Patty bit her lower lip. In the thirteen years since she had been coming to these marches, the tone had changed considerably. What used to be women gathering to demand safety on the streets on the third Friday of September had turned into a free-for-all in North America. A few years ago when the March in Toronto was held in Regent Park, the men came out and threw bottles at the women. After that, every year the violence seemed to escalate. Smaller towns and cities were cancelling their marches for fear the women would be hurt. Calgary was still a large enough city to offer protection for the women, although last year the shouting between the marchers and the men that lined the route got ugly and ended up with the police breaking up two walls of people screaming and throwing things at each other. This year the organizers dedicated themselves to non-violence. Patty ducked her head and walked under an orange and yellow banner asking, "What part of 'no' can't you understand?"

Hundreds of women were brandishing signs, carrying drums, and talking animatedly. She was proud to be part of this movement to reclaim the night, reclaim safety. There would always be radicals and weirdos, she thought, but we are doing the right thing now by marching to say how angry we are at the violence against women. Patty, along with hundreds of women that evening, wanted to express the desire to end their fear of sexual assault and victim blaming, to make the statement that women were not going to stand for it any longer.

Her eyes glazed over as she remembered nine years ago, walking home one evening after working late in the studio. She gasped as she felt hands over her mouth, strange arms clenched her own, pushed her into a car. With the gun in her face, she looked into the eyes of her attacker, deep into his ugly twisted soul. Patty still shivered when memories like these erupted, although they were coming less often now. Therapy, her partner Claire, and her support group had all helped her. She pulled the collar of her deep purple shirt up against her neck, as though it offered her extra protection.

"Patty, hi." The terrible flashback evaporated and she was back at the March.

"Hey, Lois, how's it going?"

"Okay, I guess. Looks like we're getting a good turnout today." Lois straightened her round rose-coloured glasses.

"Yeah." Patty looked over to the line of police. "I hope things go smoothly."

"Oh, don't worry, Patty. I'm a marshal this year. We all had to take workshops in non-violent intervention. We're in the 1990s now, civilization marching on and all that. Last year was just one of those things."

"And the year before?"

A woman wearing a black denim jacket jostled Lois on her way up the stairs. On the right front, she wore a large button that said: "The best way to a man's heart is . . . through his chest." On the other side of the jacket was another button: "So many men . . . so little intelligence." Her faded blue jeans and brown work boots almost completed her look; that was done by the back of her short hair, shaved in the pattern of a labrys, the double-sided axe used by lesbians as a symbol of strength and independence.

Lois looked her over disapprovingly. "Gina, aren't you afraid you're going to antagonize the men dressed like that?"

"I certainly hope so." Gina grinned, showing the gap between her two front teeth. "They definitely antagonize me."

"Look, you know that we're committed to a peaceful march this year. Why fan the flames?"

"Hey, c'mon on, Lois. I live in this city too. I need to be able to walk down the streets safely. This is me, it's how I look. If men don't like it, fuck 'em. Besides, that new action group is showing up today. I'm going to join them." Gina beamed proudly.

"What new action group?" Alerted by talk of a new group, Patty joined the conversation.

"It's dynamite, Patty. Some women from The States started it; there's this underground group called STALAG, except it's not so underground. It's an offshoot from the Lesbian Avengers in New York. It stands for Serious Thelma and Louise Action Group. Except in private, they call it the Serious Thelma and Louise Army with Guns. They all carry guns. They say we're in a war and need to be armed against attacks."

"I thought most women were still fighting for gun control laws," murmured Patty.

"Not these women. They're radical and they're not afraid to fight back. And I'm not either." Gina puffed out her chest. "Oh, I see some of them now. See ya later. Have a good march." Gina loped over to a group of women converging on the steps. Patty looked at their group and shrugged.

"They look like regular women to me. Hope they're not looking to make trouble. Oh well, I guess we each need to do what we need to do. See you later, Lois. I'm lookin' for some friends of mine."

As Patty elbowed her way to the top of the steps, she spotted Denise and Noreen just as Claire walked up to them.

"Hi Patty." Denise embraced her friend. "Beautiful evening for the March, eh?"

Patty looked at the blue sky with only a few puffy clouds. It was early evening, so still light out. That was one advantage of living in Calgary. The weather was so beautiful. Having the March on the third Friday of September almost guaranteed great weather.

"Hey, Denise, Noreen. Hi, sweetie," Patty leaned over to kiss Claire.

The four friends had been coming to the March since its Calgary inception, although Claire and Patty had not known each other well at the earlier Marches. Since the two of them got closer, the four friends had gone together for the past six years. Of all the many activities they did as a group, the March was a favourite of theirs.

Claire folded the collar of Patty's shirt down and slid her arms under Patty's jean jacket, hugging her tightly. Claire had never been one for public affection until six years ago, when she and Patty had fallen in love. Claire stood back and with Patty, looked over the sea of movement in front of them. Claire was the most subdued of the four women. Now late into her fourth decade, her hair had begun to change from light brown to a salt and pepper, providing opportunity for many compliments from friends and strangers alike. She kept it cut stylishly short; she always liked to look immaculately well-groomed and was convinced it was easier to appear neat with short hair. She did enjoy Patty's long hair, and didn't mind if Patty was tousled and disorganized, but she was meticulous about her own appearance. This showed in her fitted brown tweed blazer, khaki slacks, cream-coloured blouse tucked in, brown belt, and brown suede shoes. Patty was the antithesis; long, blonde ponytail, usually with strands of hair flying out of the band that held it together, wearing clothes that were colourful and often didn't seem to go together, although Patty swore that everything matched if one looked at it right. The two got along so wonderfully well precisely because they were so disparate.

Standing with their friends on the top of the steps to City Hall, Noreen and Denise looked very differently. Noreen had short red hair, a face full of freckles, and had a proclivity for brightly checked shirts she wore with her jeans and sneakers. She stood to the side, admiring Denise. At times she thought she could almost see a golden halo surrounding Denise's flowing dark brown hair. Without question, Noreen felt Denise was the kindest, gentlest, and most intelligent person she knew, and almost everyone who knew Denise agreed with Noreen, who felt she was the luckiest person in the world. Denise was always very well put together; she loved shopping, for both clothes and food, as she was an expert chef as well as a lover of fine apparel. She explained to Noreen that her being a therapist meant she had to look as other people thought a therapist should look, not necessarily how she would dress when on holidays and knew no one. Denise always tried to make people feel as comfortable as possible. Occasionally Noreen almost felt envious of Denise's clients. Denise was considered one of the premiere therapists in the city and had a long waiting list of people anxious to see her. Noreen shared a home with this wonderful woman for almost two decades and planned to do so for the rest of their lives.

Noreen worked with Claire, the best person with whom to hitch a work-related star, and they had become very close as well as extremely successful in their genetic research. Noreen felt truly blessed as she stood amidst her lover, colleague, and friends.

All four women had been active in the women's community since their University days, although Claire often laughingly accused her best friend Noreen of making a feminist out of her.

"Oh great, looks like we're starting." Claire linked arms with Patty and the four started down the stairs with the others.

Hundreds of women began to file into the street. The marshals were stationed every half block or so with megaphones.

"Stay on the street in your group, women," the megaphone blared. "Don't respond to taunts. Just keep marching."

Patty filed down the stairs and onto the streets chanting with all the others as the march crossed Ninth Avenue and turned right onto 11th Avenue.

Patty, Claire, Noreen, and Denise linked arms and skipped-danced as they chanted with the women:

"Yes means yes.

No means no.

Rape and violence

Have got to go."

This said in a sing-songy voice over and over, emphasizing the *go*.

They were about a quarter of the way into the march and as Patty turned back, laughing, singing, and march-dancing with her friends, she saw hundreds of women, waving signs, beating drums and chanting; she felt full of pride.

The marchers suddenly slowed and Patty looked around to see groups of men standing on the sidewalk to her right, taunting the women. She heard the marshal: "Don't respond. Ignore them. They are looking for a response."

Patty took a deep breath and tightened her hold on the arms of Denise and Claire.

"Hey, cunt, come on over here. I'll show you something to reclaim!" A large man wearing a tee shirt that blared out in bright red and yellow "kick butt" yelled out to the marshal.

"Lookit th' dykes," yelled another. "Hey, we'll fix you up. You just need some of this." He grabbed his crotch. "Come on over!"

The men roared with approval.

At first, Patty didn't know what it was. "Ow!" Something hit her shoulder. "Ow again!" Another something thwacked against the back of her leg. She turned around and saw a group of men pelting the marchers with small stones.

"Oh my god, look!"

Then the group of men moved closer towards the women. Some threw bottles, some threw larger stones. One woman fell into the crowd, a stream of blood running down her face. People began running in all directions. Patty wasn't sure what was happening.

The parade stopped. A few women knelt down to help the bleeding woman. Others started to run off the street.

"Women, stay on the street," ordered the marshal. "Don't go onto the sidewalk. Stay together. Fuck. Where are the goddamn police?!"

A shot echoed in the air and the marshal fell. Women began screaming. Men were shouting. One of the women screamed and fell, holding her side. Suddenly a group of women burst through the crowd. They stood shoulder to shoulder and began firing upon the men. Blam, blamblam. The men continued shooting. Patty was paralysed with fear. Her feet were cemented to the pavement. Wounded men lay on the sidewalk. Women were strewn in the street. Blamblam. Blam. She felt as though she were in a scary movie, that it was all unreal.

The police came barrelling down 11th Avenue, guns drawn, shields held high in front. The armed women quickly dispersed into the crowd. The men scattered.

Patty felt someone grab her arm and pull. Screams were

everywhere. The police were shouting, guns in the air. Men and women were running all over the streets and sidewalks. Bodies were lying in the street. Patty felt another tug and decided to go with her arm. She was scared to look, but more frightened not to. She heard crying, knew it wasn't her. She realized with relief that the sounds of guns firing had stopped. She almost tripped over a man's bleeding body lying across the sidewalk as she was propelled into a building by her friends. Everywhere women were crying and shouting.

"Here, Patty, sit down here." She felt Denise lower her gently onto a chair. She looked up into the strong, gentle eyes of Claire and somehow, through Claire, Patty came back into present reality.

"Where are we?"

"We're in the women's building. It's safe here. The doors are locked. We're only letting women in. It seems as though the police have everything under control now. If that's what one might call it."

Patty looked about the room and saw about twenty women, some weeping, some shouting with angry gestures, many still in a state of shock like herself. From another room, she heard the sound of voices emanating from the TV.

Patty followed her friends and sat down on the floor beside them in front of the TV. Claire had her arm around her on one side, Denise sat closely on the other side, Noreen beside her. By now, there were over one hundred women in the room, glad for the closeness, the ability to sit touching one another in safety while they watched, in amazement and disbelief, the news of the March.

SEPTEMBER 19, 1992

Next day

EXCERPT FROM CALGARY Courier Newspaper:
Violence erupted last night at a local Take Back the Night March, sponsored by the Alberta Status of Women Action Committee (ASWAC) in conjunction with the Calgary Status of Women Action Committee. The violence, which was rumoured to be started by a group of men lining the march route along 11th Ave SW, left three women dead, seven men severely injured, and numerous other non-life-threatening injuries in its wake. The rumours of how the violence started were not confirmed.

The Take Back the Night Marches have been happening around the world since the 1970s. They are thought to have originated in Philadelphia following the violent murder of Susan Alexander Speeth, a microbiologist at the university, who was brutally stabbed and left for dead while she was walking home alone at night. The following year, 1976, saw a March in Belgium during the International Tribunal on Crimes Against Women. Since then, they have been occurring annually in most big cities worldwide. In Canada, the impetus for the Marches was thought to be the 1980 brutal murder of Barbra Schlifer, who had been sexually assaulted and killed on her way home after celebrating her call to the bar. She was murdered in the basement stairwell of her Toronto apartment.

Organizers of last night's March stated they were shocked and appalled by what had transpired. Mary Kirsten, chairperson of ASWAC, and board member of the local group, told reporters that the speeches had to be cancelled after the outbreak of violence.

"We were committed to a peaceful march," Kirsten added. "All our marshals had to take non-violent-intervention workshops. We did everything we could to try to maintain peace. The men lining the route began throwing things at the women, until finally, one woman dropped in a pool of blood. After that, chaos reigned."

Kirsten was not able to comment as to whether or not a March would take place the following year.

"Those women were just asking for it," Mel "Jinky" Davis explained. Davis was one of the organizers of the men who were lining the streets along 11th Ave SW. "What did they expect? I mean, all those undesirables, you know, unmarrieds, feminists, those lezzies, all flaunting their beliefs. They were just asking for trouble. They wanted trouble, they got trouble."

Police have stated they are investigating the situation. To date, no one has been charged. "Look," explained Constable Joshua Marley, "three people have been murdered and many more have been injured. We will launch a full scale investigation into this, you can be sure of that." The police were not prepared to comment on where they felt the fault lay in the eruption of violence.

"The city is still in shock," remarked Frances Whetherby, special assistant to the Mayor, who is currently in Europe. "Our condolences go out to the families of the deceased. We send our wishes for speedy recoveries to all the injured people. We feel that for now, the city needs to recover and get over the shock of what has happened."

OCTOBER 8, 1992

Three weeks later

"GOOD EVENING, LADIES, thank you all for coming. My name is Ann and I'll be the facilitator for the evening. This is a brainstorming meeting for the monument project, a project that was originated to honour the women massacred in Montreal at the School of Engineering three years ago and which now has expanded to honour all women who are victims of male violence. You have an agenda in your packet, but first of all, I'd like to start off the evening by having everyone in the circle introduce herself and say why she is here. I'll start with myself. My name, as I said, is Ann, Ann Flother, and I work here at the Old Y. For those of you who may not know, the Old Y is where most of the women's community organizations are situated, like the Status of Women, the Birth Control Association, and many others. I've been involved with the committee for this project from the beginning. I've agreed to act as facilitator here tonight."

Patty leaned against the wall in her chair and looked around the room. "Wow," she murmured, "what a mixture of women." Gathered in the room were many women dressed, as Patty later described to her friends, in dress for success clothes. There was a sprinkling of jeans and Birkenstocks and an eclectic mix of others as well.

Patty listened as the women went around the circle introducing themselves. There was an executive from the office of women's affairs, a representative from a cabinet minister's office, a banker, an insurance woman, and several professional fundraisers. Many said they were asked to attend the meeting because of their expertise in these roles. When it came to Patty's turn, she said she was an artist and was there because of personal interest. She left out all the work she had done in the feminist community for the last quarter of a century. First, she wanted to observe this group.

Following the introductions, Cris, whom Patty had worked with for years at the old Y, showed a slide show of other monuments to honour the dead. Patty loved watching slides of The Dinner Party, the AIDS Quilt, the Vietnam Memorial. Cris had added music to the slides. It was a very moving presentation.

Then Julie gave a report on what had been done to date by the committee.

"We already have approval in principal for the site, but we are not in agreement with the city over the inscription. We think the inscription should read in part "for women murdered by men" but the city finds "by men" discriminatory."

"Oh, I agree completely with the city. I find it very objectionable." Patty looked over at the woman in a rust skirt, beige blouse with a little jacket, golden silk scarf, and too much makeup on her face.

"Sometimes it's better not to say anything. It's stronger by what is left unsaid." This from a woman across from her who was wearing a neat yellow dress.

"Oh, I agree," added a third. "We don't want to antagonize the men."

The conversation went along in that vein until Patty could no longer sit still.

"Excuse me, excuse me," she shouted, waving her arm in the air. "You women are doing exactly what this monument is trying to circumvent—you are erasing history. These women were killed by men. It is a fact, not a discriminatory statement. Look at the statistics. By not saying that, we will be playing right into the society that created the conditions for all these women to be slaughtered in the first place. Remember the Montreal Massacre just a few years ago? And how about the March just a few weeks ago in this very city? How quickly we forget. Women were killed by men, and we should say that."

"Oh no, no, no," exclaimed a woman in a dark red suit. "We will never be able to raise funds if we say that. We must make it easy for men to give money to this project."

"Look," shouted Patty, "you are being co-opted just like everyone else. The men should give money because it was men who murdered women and they have a sense of moral responsibility, not because we flatter them so they think they are doing us a favour and helping the little ladies."

Ms. Rust Skirt spoke again, smiling pleasantly at Patty. "I have a lot of experience fund raising, dear, and you simply won't be able to raise money this way. As a rule of thumb, you need to have the involvement of the people giving the money; you don't want to alienate them. I'm sure you would understand this when you are more familiar with fundraising."

Patty glanced at Cris and then at Ann, both of whom knew her proven capabilities of raising money for unpopular causes. They smiled at one another.

"We must figure out a way to give the people something for contributing," the woman continued.

"Look," Patty sat forward in her chair, "do you even know where that expression you just used, 'rule of thumb,' came from? It comes from British Common Law in the eighteenth century, where it was stated that a man was allowed to beat his wife, or rather offer her 'moderate correction,'" Patty emphasized this by making air quotation marks with her fingers, "as long as the stick used for beating was no wider that the thickness of the man's thumb. I bring this up now to illustrate how insidious all this violence against women is. Indeed it has infiltrated our society today, when a good woman such as yourself can use an expression like this and not even be aware of its origin, or what it meant to those poor women who were regularly being beaten." Patty sat back in her chair and took a deep breath.

"Look, no one is beating anyone here," Ms. Yellow Dress replied. "The committee doesn't want to discriminate; every donor, no matter what the amount, would be inscribed on the monument."

Ms. Red Suit turned to Patty. "You need to bribe the men and appeal to their egos."

"No!" Patty cried out. "This is a women's project, so maybe we should find women's ways to deal with it and not do everything the boys' ways."

Ms. Red Suit looked over her glasses at Patty. "Don't take all this so personally, my dear."

"I do take it personally, and I'm not your dear, my name is Patty."

Patty sat tall in her chair. "And I take it politically too. The personal is the political. Isn't that what it means to be a feminist?"

"Oh, I'm not a feminist, Patty." Ms. Red Suit emphasized "Patty" in a sharp, unfriendly way. "Now, Patty, you can hold your bake sales, but you won't get much money that way."

"That's not what I mean," countered Patty. "But surely we can motivate the people of Canada to contribute to a national monument honouring victims of male violence by other means, like a belief in safety for women and a sense of need for the community."

Patty looked around the room. "And for all of you who say you're not feminists—do you not believe in equality for everyone? For that is what a feminist is. How can you believe that you are not as equal as the men around you? If you believe you are, then you are a feminist."

"We are getting a little off track here," Ann interrupted. "Perhaps we should have our financial report now."

Two hours later, a very frustrated Patty hugged Cris and Ann good night and made her way back home. She sat in her studio, thinking for another hour and a half. She thought that Rebecca West really had it right when she said, "I only know that people call me a feminist whenever I express sentiments that differentiate me from a doormat." That was in 1913 and it was now 1992. Patty wondered if things were ever really going to change for women.

OCTOBER 17, 1992

Ten days later

NOREEN DROPPED THE napkins quickly around the table set for four and looked around. She loved this house, which she and Denise had bought fourteen years ago.

They referred to it as their little log cabin, because essentially that's what it was when they first bought it. It still was a log cabin, although now considerably larger and much more contemporary after their renovation eight years ago.

It sat on five acres on a large hill on the southwest side of Calgary, overlooking the city, the river, the University and the research labs, and when outside, if one turned around, she could see the snow-capped mountains off in the distance.

She heard the front door open.

"Hi, come on in." She smiled and with a slight but exaggerated bow, indicated with a sweep of her hand the way to the large living room, where a fire was burning invitingly in the floor-to-ceiling stone fireplace.

Claire and Patty each hugged her on their way into the house.

"Where's Denise?"

"Oh, she's in the kitchen, no doubt preparing some culinary delights. C'mon in."

They walked down the hall into the living room.

"So, what have you two been up to?"

Claire and Patty plopped down onto the plush, harvest gold sofa, pushing aside the orange and yellow pillows.

"Oh, y'know, the usual. Patty's been painting up a storm."

"Yeah, I have done a lot of new work," added Patty, "and we've both been watching the olds on the telly. It's no longer the news, it's always the same old things. Rape, murder, abuse; it's disgusting. How about you?"

"Oh, 'bout the same. Wasn't that March something? I couldn't believe what I was watching on TV and we were there. Denise has been working on her latest paper all week when she could concentrate on that and not fixate on the damn March. It's been weeks already, and it's still in the news. People being shot at and killed is not very common in Calgary. We'll be hearing about that for a long time I think. And . . . we've been quite busy at work these days too."

"Tell me about it." Claire grimaced.

"Hey, what's this?" Patty picked up a magazine which was lying on the coffee table in front of her.

"Oh, that's very cool. *Herizons*, a new Canadian Feminist news magazine. You can borrow it if you like. We've both finished reading it. It's so great to have a Canadian version of *Ms*, but better I think. So, how about some wine? Or something else?"

"White wine is fine, thanks Nori." Patty flipped through *Herizons* with great interest.

"Wine for me too, please."

Denise entered from a door on the far side of the living room. Her long dark hair tumbled down her back. She carried in a plate of pâté and crackers. She wore a beautiful patchwork jacket in muted colours which hung loosely over black silk pants. "Hi, gang. How are you two tonight?"

"Great, Denny. You look very elegant this evening. What's this?" Patty grabbed a cracker and swooped up some pâté. "Umm good, I'm starving. What is this, anyway?"

"Salmon pâté. I just found it today at Pepper's, on 17th Avenue."

"Well, it's delicious. Denny, you always find such interesting things. Here, honey, have some." Patty put some on a cracker and handed it to Claire.

"Thanks." Claire took a tiny bite off a corner of the cracker, thoughtfully chewed it, decided it was delicious and then popped the rest into her mouth. She then wiped off the few crumbs that had fallen onto her new brown ultra-suede blazer and leaned back into the sofa. She felt comfortable in this room. After all, she and Noreen had been friends for over twenty years. They first met in graduate school when they were working together on their PhDs. Claire was working on a project in biochemical genetics and Noreen was doing a project on immunology and genetics. They became fast friends, finishing their PhDs the same year. They were very lucky when that year a large amount of money was allocated to genetic and biochemical research and they were both hired as researchers for the Heritage Foundation, working out of the University of Calgary. Initially, they worked in the same department in charge of different projects. More recently, they had joined forces and had become partners in their work in genetics and biochemical immunology. Claire looked around the familiar room—from the start it had always been a welcoming, comfortable place to be, and Claire spent a lot of time there.

"So, Patty, have you recovered from the March yet?" Denise asked.

"Yeah. These Take Back The Night things are getting too violent for me. Remember when we used to be able to do it and just march down the street? Then a few years ago in Toronto in Regent Park they started throwing bottles at the women and now it's like target practice for any bozohead."

"I know." Denise slowly shook her head. "Three fatalities and so many people injured—that's so difficult to even comprehend."

In spite of the sad start to the conversation, the evening passed very pleasurably, with delectable food, drink, and dialogue. Over the cappuccinos, Noreen turned to Claire.

"So, what d'you think about all that shit coming from Clovis' lab?"

"Gee, I don't know. It sure is causing a big upset in the department."

"What? What's happening?" Patty picked up another slice of Brie.

"Y'know the guy in the lab down the hall, Dr. Cleve Clovis . . ."

"Yeah, the one who's as stupid as his name." Patty laughed.

"That's the one." Claire chuckled. "Apparently they may have isolated something that has a predilection for Sertoli cells and . . ."

"Hey c'mon, you scientists," Patty punctuated the air with her fork, "speak so we mere mortals can understand. Who's Sir Toby?"

"Not Sir Toby. Sertoli, Sertoli cells, the cells that sperm have."

"Sperm. Yuck. Who cares about sperm? I haven't seen any for twenty years."

"Well, Clovis cares about sperm," Claire responded. "Maybe we should call what's happening with the sperm The Y Syndrome."

Noreen snorted in delight.

"You would think they were doing genetic biodetermination experiments there," Claire continued, "everything is so hush hush. But it seems like maybe they found something they weren't looking for, that might be killing off the sperm."

"Oh well, that I can handle." Patty laughed. "Maybe they can start with the US Supreme Court and then nominate Anita Hill. And then they can get the sperm of all the rapists, and then . . ."

"Patty." There was a hint of exasperation in Claire's voice.

"Wait a minute," Denny interjected. "Are you trying to tell me that there's something that will kill sperm? And if that's the case, will it kill men? That's unbelievable."

"Well, we don't know. We only know that there's a lot of mystery going on in that lab and it has something to do with Sertoli cells and an unwanted effect, perhaps a virus, as Claire says, we'll call it The Y Syndrome," Patty turned and smiled at Claire, "but they don't know what's going on yet."

"Wow," mused Denise, "wouldn't that be something? Imagine getting a hold of that virus."

"We don't even know for sure if it is a virus. Besides, that could be quite dangerous. For all of us. Including Clovis." Claire placed her fork down and arranged it exactly perpendicular to the edge of the table.

"Okay, I have a question." Patty put down her glass. "If this Clovis is so stupid, how come he is Dr. Clovis? Don't you have to be a little bit smart to get a doctorate?"

"I remember him from graduate school." Claire turned to Patty. "He didn't seem that stupid then but he was not very smart around people; he just didn't get people the way that we do."

"Like how?" Patty asked. "Give me an example."

"Well, let's see." Claire deliberated for a few seconds. "He doesn't seem to be able to read people. He can be talking about something, sometimes going on and on and on, and he seems to have no idea if people are even interested, or he can't tell if they are bored or not. He just can't seem to tell how people are feeling, or what they might want. Or need. If you tell him, he tries to act appropriately, but he really can't figure it out on his own. He's very literal.

"Here's something else he often does. Say a student, or anyone really, is walking down the hall struggling with an armful of lab equipment, or books, or anything. If Nori or I saw them, we'd offer to help. With Clovis, that would never cross his mind. But if I said, 'Cleve, give us a hand with this,' he would always say 'sure, of course,' and would be quite happy to do it. It just would never occur to him to help other people. Those are just a few examples, but there are many more."

Noreen laughed. "I always thought of him as sort of a wishy-washy guy. He wasn't that bad but he wasn't that good. He managed to get his PhD because he got very lucky. When all of us were in graduate school, in the late '60s, early '70s, genetics was a hot topic. DNA was a big thing and everyone wanted to work in genetics. One of the professors was working on quite an innovative experiment, and Clovis somehow got assigned to his lab as a new grad student."

"That's right," Claire kicked in. "That was Professor Wellington. Clovis worked in his lab, helping him. He did that for almost two years, I think, right, Nori?"

Noreen nodded.

"After two years, Dr. Wellington had a stroke. And somehow Clovis stayed in his lab, doing Wellington's work, and used it for his PhD thesis." Claire made sure her knife was exactly perpendicular to the table.

"That's right," Noreen continued. "Clovis just kept right on working in Wellington's lab. At the time, we wondered how he could even get away with using Wellington's work for his thesis, but I guess since he had been working in that lab anyway, it seemed appropriate for him to use the work that they did in the lab."

"And," Claire continued, "he had been working with Wellington in his lab for two years so ostensibly he had contributed *something* to the work. So he became Dr. Clovis about the same time we got our doctorates. And there you have it."

"Y'know, we need to find out more about what's going on in that lab of his." Noreen scratched her head. "We have a right to know."

"Ah, you know they keep it locked up tightly. They don't let anyone in, even when they are there."

"Hmmm. All the more reason to find out what's going on in there. Let's do some detective work next week, okay?"

"I don't know. I think we should leave their lab alone. I sure wouldn't want anyone coming into our lab and messing up the research." Claire brushed back her hair.

"Yeah, but that's different."

"Look, you two scientists work it out next week. C'mon, let's go sit in the living room and get that fire going again."

"Great idea, Denny. I'll help you clear." Patty leapt up, her hands full of dishes.

HOURS LATER, NOREEN and Denise were getting ready for bed.

"Well, that was another enjoyable evening, don't you think?" Noreen looked up at Denise as she pulled back the sheets. "I sure enjoy our time with those two."

"Hmm. I do too. Honey?"

"What?" Noreen slipped under the brightly coloured quilt on their bed.

"Do you really think there's something that can kill sperm?"

"I don't know. But I think we'll do a bit more checking up about Clovis' lab. This conversation tonight has piqued my interest."

"And mine. Just like you do." Denise enfolded Noreen in her arms.

OCTOBER 30, 1992

Two weeks later

"CLAIRE!" NOREEN BURST into their office on the third floor of the Science Building.

Claire looked up from the files on her desk. "Oh, you frightened me."

"There really is something funny going on in that lab."

"What lab? You mean Clovis' lab?"

"Yeah. There are men in there today. They don't look like scientists; they look more like cops if you ask me. Wrinkled suits, ties, if you know what I mean."

Claire rubbed her forehead. "I think you're making a big deal about this. Clovis isn't even a good scientist. What could he possibly have?"

"I don't know, but I'm sure going to find out. Will you help me?"

"C'mon, you can't be serious. Let's just do our work."

Noreen plopped down on the chair next to Claire's desk. "I feel this is important. Something's going on in there that we need to know about. Stay late with me tonight and we'll check it out. If it seems like his usual dumb work, we'll just leave and call it quits. Okay?"

"Well, maybe." Claire remembered many years ago when she was working in exciting new developments and her lab was up for a large grant. Clovis managed to divert the funds into his lab at the last minute, then never produced anything of much interest. That had all happened before she shared work space with Noreen.

"Okay, sure. We'll just look around a bit." Claire was grateful that they were together at work. One of the main reasons they preferred to work in the same office and lab was that they continually consulted one another. Looking around, she realised that she loved the large room.

She smiled when she saw the two desks. Her desk was immaculate, with everything exactly where it belonged, while Noreen's was a disaster area of open books, papers lying all over the place, and not one millimeter of clear desk space visible.

Their lab was off to the right, with three long counters, six feet width between them. On the counters were beakers, test tubes, lab equipment everywhere. Six desks were spread out along the length of the right wall, used by graduate students. At the far end was another door that led out to the main third floor hall.

The windows above the six desks allowed light to stream into the lab, giving it a most pleasant feeling. It was inviting and not overwhelming at all. Claire and Noreen were both proud of the space they designed.

After they had each done impressive work the same year, bringing accolades to the University and increased grant money for their individual work, the university had agreed to build them a combined work space. Neither one had regretted that move for even one second.

IT WAS NOT unusual for either Noreen or Claire to be in the lab late at night so when Leo the security guard came around, he greeted them in his usual fashion.

"Well, doctors, working late again, eh?"

"Yeah, we are." Noreen looked up. "Hey, I was in Dr. Clovis' lab earlier today and left my notebook in there. Would you open that lab for me, please, Leo? I need to get my stuff back."

"Gee, Dr. Stanton, I have very strict orders not to open his lab for anyone at any time. Sorry, but no can do." Leo ran his hand through his curly black hair.

"Strange orders. What's the big deal?" Claire tried to look casual as she leaned back in her chair.

"Don't know, Dr. Christopher. Just got those orders today. I guess there were some bigwigs around earlier. Something is happening there, but I don't know what. Sorry I can't help you."

"That's okay, Leo. I'll get my notebook tomorrow."

Leo left the room, and Noreen gave Claire a quizzical look.

"See, I told you," Noreen whispered. "I know there's some hanky-panky going on there and I'm going to find out what it is."

"Yeah, I'm pretty curious too. So, how are we going to do this?"

Noreen fiddled with the large multi-coloured model of DNA on her desk. She often did that when she was thinking.

Claire leaned far back in her chair and looked up at the ceiling. She started counting squares, although she already knew there were eight large sections and sixteen smaller squares in each of the eight. At times of intense concentration, she had even counted the tiny dots in each square. Noreen followed her gaze and looked at the ceiling, then jumped up on her chair.

"What are you doing?" Claire asked as Noreen moved aside papers to stand on her desk.

"Look." Noreen pushed up one of the small squares. "We can get in through the ceiling."

"Oh, don't be ridiculous."

"No, really, look. We just go to the nearest room near Clovis' lab, climb up through the ceiling, see it's really a fake ceiling, and then plop down in his lab. We won't even use the door. And then we'll leave the same way and no one will ever know. Come on, let's do it."

"What if Leo comes?"

"Oh, he won't be around for another hour at least. Come on, for heaven's sake. Let's go." Noreen was already out the door.

Clovis' lab was in the southeast corner of the building. Across the south wall were the washrooms, first the men's and then the women's.

Noreen surveyed the situation. "Well, I guess we need to try going in through the men's washroom."

Claire gave the door to the men's washroom a doubtful look. "Oh, this is getting ridiculous."

"We need to find out what's going on in there. Come on. Everyone has gone home now. We can think up some dumb excuse if we're caught." Noreen hoped that was true.

Inside the men's washroom were three cubicles and three urinals across from them.

Claire grimaced. "This is so distasteful."

"Yeah, I know, aren't urinals yucky?"

"I wasn't talking about the urinals."

"Look, I think if I stand on the back of this toilet and you help me, I can get up on the crossbar of the ceiling. See? It'll be easy. Here, here are the squares." Noreen handed the corrugated tiles down to Claire. "I can get though here now. Just stand on the toilet and give me a boost. I'll check things out and let you know."

"Noreen Stanton, this is about the dumbest thing we have ever done."

"Right. Now give me a boost. Ooph." Noreen struggled to pull herself up to the steel crossbars.

"Be careful."

"Yeah, yeah, I'm careful. Okay, I'm up here. I'm going to crawl across these crossbars, hope they don't break, and hop into Clovis' lab. Then I'll open the door for you. You put the tiles back now and I'll meet you in the hall. It's okay, go."

Claire sighed, and standing on the toilet, replaced the tiles. She looked around the washroom, making sure that they hadn't left anything out of place, and then eased out the door. She waited in the hall in front of the lab door for what seemed like an eternity. She heard the men's washroom door open, and out came Noreen.

"Nori! What . . . ?"

"You won't believe this. There's this fake ceiling everywhere except over the lab. It's totally closed off with solid metal. There's absolutely no way to get in there. I can't believe it."

They looked at each other.

"Now we *really* need to find out what's going on in there," Noreen proclaimed.

Claire nodded in agreement as they headed back down the hall.

NOVEMBER 2, 1992

Three days later

"CLAIRE, CLAIRE!" PATTY yelled as she ran into the house, blond ponytail flying. She slammed the door shut, slipped out of her red down vest, and left it lying on the floor.

"Claire! Where are you?"

"Right here, I'm right here. What's up?" Claire picked up the vest and hung it in the closet.

"The gallery wants to do my show. Just me. How cool is that?"

"Oh, sweetie, tell me all about it." Claire put her arm around Patty and led her to the sofa in the living room.

"It's the Haines Gallery. I knew they were kinda interested in my work, but wow—I was so surprised. I went in to see them. You know, a new gallery in town so I wanted to see if they would show my work occasionally. They told me they had been thinking about me and would like to do a show. And they'll show my work all the time after that. I'm so excited. And . . . and they have enough space to show the really big ones too."

"Oh, honey, I'm delighted. I'm so pleased for you, I really am." Claire looked at the huge oil painting, five feet square, of clouds in the sky and off in the distance, a beautiful landscape of grasses blowing in the wind, on the wall over the living room entrance. The colours were subdued, yet strong.

"I just love that piece, so peaceful."

"Yeah, I like it too. I did that one for you. For us. For our home. That's why it's so special."

"That's one advantage of living with an artist." Claire smiled. "We have so many awesome paintings on the walls."

They looked around the living room. Paintings, mostly done by Patty, hung on every wall. The furniture, the sofa, love seat, and two overstuffed armchairs were inviting and the whole room had a very comfortable feel. They had decorated it together when they first moved there six years ago and they loved it even more now.

The house was just off Elbow Drive, backed onto the river, and they had been very lucky to find it. It was an older house, well maintained and fully renovated just before they bought it and was perfect for the two of them. An artist had owned it previously, so Patty moved right into the studio that seemed to have been built for her, as some of her pieces were quite as large as the previous owner's. Claire had the perfect study toward the back of the house where others rarely wandered, which suited her well. She was extremely particular as to where her things belonged.

They lounged in silence for a few minutes, each thinking the very same thoughts—how lucky they both were to be sharing this wonderful home together. Claire cherished Patty's spontaneity, her liveliness, her unpredictable nature; Patty treasured the stability that Claire brought to her life, her wisdom and her quiet gentility.

"I love your hair. It's so beautiful." Patty rubbed Claire's thick salt-and-pepper hair, cut stylishly short.

"Oh, don't be ridiculous. It's just plain hair."

"Yeah, but it's so neat. And it goes so well with the painting."

Claire laughed, took Patty's hand off her head, kissed it, and held it in her lap.

"And what have you been up to today?" Patty asked.

"Well, y'know Noreen is so distracted about that whole Clovis thing that it's impossible to get her to do any work at all. If she's not snooping down the hall, she's talking about it. It seems as though I've lost my work partner." Claire straightened a candy dish on the coffee table so it was precisely in the centre.

"Well, she'll come 'round soon. You know Noreen, it's always something."

"Well, I don't know." Claire sighed. "This seems like something bigger. I have to say, I'm a bit concerned about what's going on there as well. We'll just have to see what the next little while brings. But enough about that. Tell me more about the gallery."

NOVEMBER 4, 1992

Two days later

NOREEN WHEELED INTO an empty space in the parking lot and quickly hopped out of her little orange sports car. She gathered all her papers, which always seemed to be falling out of her briefcase, and with her arms full, kicked the door shut with her foot and headed towards the Science Building.

She backed into a body. "Ooph, excuse me. Oh, Cleve, hi. How're you doing?"

"Hello, Stanton. Nice day, isn't it?"

"Yeah, it is, Cleve. Is that yours?" She nodded at a metallic brown Cadillac Seville parked next to her little Fiat.

"Yep, sure is. Beauty, isn't it?" Clovis grinned.

"It is," Noreen agreed. "So, what's new?"

"Oh, y'know. Nothing much."

"I see you've had a bit of action around your lab lately," Noreen said tentatively.

"Action? What do you mean, action? What do you mean? There's no action." Clovis hurried up his pace.

"Cleve, wait. I'm just interested. You're always working on such interesting projects. What're you up to these days?"

"Can't tell you. Confidential."

"Oh for heaven's sake, what could be confidential about your lab?"

"Big things. Can't say." Clovis puffed up his chest.

"You're looking quite spiffy these days." Noreen nudged her head at Clovis' chocolate suede jacket, tan pressed pants, and crisp cream sport shirt. "Win the lottery or something?"

"Just doing what all good scientists do. Going where the money is." He winked at her.

"And I don't suppose you would want to share where that might be?"

"Nope. Sort of an old boys' thing, y'know." He held the door open for her.

"Oh, no, after *you*."

"If you insist. You feminists are all alike. Can't stand to have anyone be nice to you." Cleve Clovis turned down the hall to his lab.

Noreen barely hesitated before following him. "Say, maybe you're right. Would you like to have coffee maybe and discuss it?"

"Aw, c'mon, Stanton, don't suck up. Discuss what?" Clovis opened his door.

Noreen stood in the doorway and glanced around. The lab, which used to be one large room, now had a wall. They stood in an anteroom with a door straight ahead, which led to the actual lab.

"Whoa, done some renovations, I see."

"Yep, just a bit. Can't be too careful about who steals your work these days."

"C'mon. We've worked together for decades. The only stealing has been done by you." Noreen immediately regretted this indiscretion.

Clovis bit his lower lip. His thick wavy brown hair, barely graying at the temples, was freshly cut. He looked good, like a nice person even, Noreen thought. Amazing how deceptive looks could be. Noreen remembered what he had done to Claire, how he had appropriated her work, and she remembered how he had deliberately misled their department head about her own work. She had straightened that out eventually, but had lost funding because of it. And now before her stood Cleve Clovis, arms crossed over his stylish new sports jacket, leaning against the inner door, smiling at her.

"Don't you have to be somewhere?" he asked.

"Yeah, I guess I do." Noreen turned and walked out the door.

NOREEN STOOD AT her desk, sorting out her papers, lost in thought, when Claire walked in..

"I don't know how anyone could function surrounded by such a mess." Claire walked to her desk and stood beside her.

"Well, at least I'm not compulsively neat like you are." Noreen smiled.

"I just bumped into Sanderson," Claire said as she sat down at her desk.

"Oh yeah? And what's the head of our Science Department up to these days?" Noreen stopped sorting.

"I asked him what all the excitement was at Cleve's lab. You know what he said? He said 'Excitement? What excitement?' So I said, 'C'mon, Tom, what's going on?' He told me nothing was going on, that it looked like Cleve might have stumbled upon something big, and they were just going to make sure before announcing it and we would all hear about it in due time. He talked to me like I was a student, not a colleague."

Noreen sat down beside Claire. "I bumped into Cleve this morning. Literally, actually. He's up to something, that's for sure. He's wearing expensive clothes, good clothes, and driving a new Cadillac, for heaven's sake. He's getting money from somewhere, I know that. Oh, and I walked right into his lab with him, hoping to take a quick look around, but you know what they've done?"

"What?"

"They walled off the main part of the lab. Now when you walk in, there's just another door. I need to find out what's going on. How can we do it?"

Claire drummed her fingers on the desk. "Let's see. Cleve is dumb, and he steals work. We know he has no real ethics. Who would be paying him off? Who would know what's going on in this building?"

"Doris!" they shouted together. They burst out laughing.

As the assistant to Dr. Sanderson, head of the entire department, Doris knew everything. In fact, they often joked that she ran the department, and not Tom Sanderson. Doris liked the two women, and often had her coffee breaks with them. What Noreen and Claire missed hearing in the men's locker room and lounge, they often heard from Doris.

Noreen picked up the phone. "Doris?" Hi. It's Noreen and Claire. What're you doing for lunch today?"

Claire smiled at Noreen and nodded.

THE THREE WOMEN got out of Claire's sedan and walked into the restaurant. Claire and Noreen had already decided they should eat away from the grounds of the complex. They wanted Doris to feel comfortable talking to them.

They often came to the HiBall Restaurant for a quick fix of excellent Cantonese food. It was near the labs and the university, but just far away that it afforded them some respite from work. The owner and waiters knew them well and in minutes their lunch had been ordered.

"So, Doris, how's Jack? And how're the kids?"

"Oh fine," Doris answered and went on to tell them all the latest news in her family. Noreen thought that Doris looked good today. Her medium-length black hair was stylishly done, her long fingernails were a bright red, she wore a soft pink silk blouse with a purple scarf around her neck, a form fitting black skirt. She looked happy and healthy.

Doris smiled at Noreen and Claire. When Jack was drinking and destroying his family, over ten years ago, these two women stood beside her. They convinced her to go to Al-Anon. In fact, she recalled, they went with her to the first two meetings. Then she helped Jack get started in AA, and things have been wonderful for the last eight years. It took Jack a while to get stabilized, but his eighth AA birthday took place last month.

After they happily slurped up their wonton soup, Noreen picked up her chopsticks and clicked them together. Claire and Doris looked at her quizzically. She picked up a small spare rib with her chopsticks, bit into it, and cleared her throat.

"Doris, do you know what is going on in Cleve's lab?"

Doris smiled. "I figured that's what you two wanted to talk with me about. I'm just amazed it's taken you so long to ask me about it."

"Well," Claire leaned forward, "what?"

"C'mon, what is going on there?" Noreen spit out the rib bone.

"You know, really, I don't know all that much."

Noreen groaned.

"No, really, it's true," Doris said. "There is something fishy going on there for sure, but it seems to be one big secret."

"Aw, c'mon, you know everything around here. We know that." Noreen grabbed another rib.

"Look, I'll just tell you what I know. I do know some. But we're not having this conversation, okay? Okay?" She grabbed Noreen's and Claire's arms and put just a little pressure on them. "I'll lose my job if Sanderson ever finds out that I've been talking with you. Or to anyone. He swore me to secrecy and told me this was extremely confidential. I promised I wouldn't tell anyone what I knew. So I'm not telling you anything now, okay?"

"Yeah, yeah, okay, of course. You know we wouldn't say anything, even under torture." Noreen smiled.

"Don't worry. We understand. We just want to know what is going on." Claire patted Doris' hand.

"Well, this is what I know, so far. It seems that Cleve was approached by the government . . ."

"Wait a minute. Our government? This government approached Cleve?"

"Noreen, hush, let her talk."

"Yes, Noreen, our government. The Canadian government. Specifically the army."

"The army. Holy shit."

"Noreen," Claire said. "Be quiet for a sec."

"Yes, the army. Well, first they came to Sanderson. They had some meetings. I don't really know what they were about, because he didn't dictate anything then for me to type out for him. The second time they came, Cleve was at the meeting. Tom was all puffed up when he came out, acting all important like he does, telling me he'd have extra work for me, all that bullshit. Like I should be impressed."

They all smiled at the image of Tom Sanderson.

"He's a pompous fool, isn't he?" Noreen said.

"Well, he sure acts like one at times," Doris replied. "So anyway, they had another meeting after that. And I did get some dictation. Just before that meeting, Sanderson took me into his office, closed the door, and swore me to secrecy. He told me the army had a special project for our department, but only he and Clovis would know about it for now. He said it was a matter of utmost security and it was only because I had been working there for him for all those years that he felt he could trust me. He told me I was not to discuss any of this with *anyone* else from the department. 'Anyone,' he said again. I knew he meant you two. But I nodded and told him not to worry about me."

"You're so cool," Claire said. "We just love you."

"I love you too. Both of you. I really mean it. I would never be telling you any of this if I didn't feel I could trust you. But to tell you the truth, I was going to come to you soon anyway and tell you all about this because I think something really strange is going on. I'm worried and I wanted your help."

"We're here for you. Carry on. What happened after the meeting with Sanderson?" Noreen held her chopsticks poised in mid-air. This story was better than eating. At least for a minute.

"So then I had to type some documents to do with research projects in Cleve's lab. One was about producing XY gametes. They were making XY genetic cells from ova and sperm and these were supposed to go over to the in vitro lab to be grown."

"Wait a minute. Are you talking about making just boy babies? What about XX? What happened to those?"

"Oh, the XX ones were destroyed and the XY ones were to be nourished. And get this—the XY ones were all going to Travell's lab where they would be grown into test tube babies, sort of. But here's the worst part—all of these studies were being done by the army."

"Wow," Claire muttered. "I see. They want to make military men by in vitro fertilization. And then likely augmenting that to make super soldiers. Wow." She couldn't stop shaking her head.

Noreen put down her chopsticks. "We started calling the work with sperm in Clovis' lab The Y Syndrome as a joke, but I don't think this sounds very funny now. Let's see if I got this straight. The army approached our government to come to our place to figure out a way to make boy babies only so they could have more soldiers? That can't be right."

"Well, they didn't put it like *that*," Doris said. "They aren't saying anything about soldiers at all. They are saying they're just doing research on fertilization and for the time being, in order to simplify, they want to direct their energies to XY only and ignore XX, for the time being, they say. They don't say anything about making only males, but if you read between the lines, that's what it really means."

"Oh, great," Noreen said, "just what this world needs. More testosterone."

"At first I didn't get it," Doris continued. "I thought because we were such a famous research institute, it was natural for the government to come to us for a special project. I couldn't figure out what all the secrecy was about, but I thought that was just government stuff. But now, I'm worried. You know, they've sealed off Clovis' lab?"

"Yeah, we know." Noreen told Doris of their escapade the week before. All three laughed until tears rolled down their faces.

"It's not funny." Claire couldn't stop laughing.

"It's hysterical. Imagine, all those boys wanting to make more boys. It's beyond belief hysterical." Noreen shook her head.

Doris dabbed at her eyes so she wouldn't ruin her perfectly applied makeup. She pushed her shiny, black hair off her face. "But here's the strange thing. Just a few weeks ago, Clovis came in all in a snit, demanding to see Sanderson right away. They had this meeting and that night Clovis' lab was sealed off. It was done at night, in secret. I don't know why. And every day, Clovis comes in to meet with Sanderson and the other day, the army types were at the meeting too. I don't know what all that is about."

"I don't suppose you have a key to Cleve's lab, do you?" Noreen asked hopefully.

"No, I don't. I know that Cleve has one and Sanderson has one, but he keeps it hidden somewhere. Even West and Cloud don't have keys."

Noreen smiled at the image of West and Cloud, Cleve's two researchers, whom Claire and she often referred to as TweedleDee and TweedleDumber.

"What does your fortune cookie say?" Noreen opened hers up.

"Mine says, 'You will find true love and happiness.' I already have." Doris smiled as she thought of Jack.

"Let's see, mine says 'Trust not in triumphs.' Hmm, wonder what that means?" Claire nibbled thoughtfully on the cookie.

"Mine says," Noreen said, "oh, get this, you won't believe it, it says. 'You are about to embark on a great adventure.'"

"You made that up."

"Yeah okay, I did. It says 'Luck is waiting around the corner.' Who's corner? Where?" Noreen laughed and popped the cookie into her mouth.

NOVEMBER 14, 1992

Ten days later

FANNY FELT THE sun on her face as she lay in bed, just beginning to awaken. She smiled as the warm rays covered her face. She could hear lively chirping coming from Bunjie, her little parakeet, swaying on a swing in the cage in the kitchen.

"Good morning, Bunjie. Isn't it going to be a beautiful winter day today?" She shook the covers off, slowly sat on the edge of the bed, lifted herself up, and trundled off toward the bathroom.

Once she was dressed and sitting at the kitchen table drinking her cocoa, she looked up at Bunjie.

"What should I do today, Bunjie? I feel the need for an adventure."

"Chirrup, cheep," replied the yellow and green bird, who had a little blue feather tuft on his head, like a hat.

"I wish I could take you with me," she wistfully said, "but then I do like having you here when I come home so there is someone I can talk to about my day. And I like that you are my guard bird and watch over the house."

"Chippie cheep," Bunjie answered.

Fanny put on her sweater, pinned on her hat, grabbed her winter coat, and put her small brown pocketbook over her arm.

"Have a good day, Bunjie. I'll see you later." The front door clicked as it locked behind her.

"Cheerup, cheep." The lilting sound of the bird singing followed her down the hall and into the street.

FANNY LOVED TO walk. Even though she was in her eighth decade, she had the strength and stamina of someone half her age. She loved to walk because she loved to look at people. And vehicles. And flowers. And buildings. In short, she loved to look at anything the world had to offer her. At times, after walking an hour or more, she would sit on a bench at a bus stop and watch the world unfold before her. One of her favourite games was making up stories about the people she observed. The stories were quite complicated and often involved two or three of the other people on the street. Then she returned home and told Bunjie all about these people and what they had ostensibly done. Her life felt full.

Sitting on her bench in the sunshine, Fanny realized she was not more than a twenty minute walk away from her friend Merle's place. Merle and Fanny had been friends for over fifty years. They attended university together. Fanny studied English and philosophy and Merle was a scientist, studying chemistry and physics. After graduation, Merle got a job in a medical research lab developing chemicals for new drugs and after a very successful career of almost fifty years, recently retired.

Fanny had always admired Merle, a tall striking woman, with short hair that had been light blonde in younger years and was now a lustrous silver. Merle always seemed to know everyone in the city. Fanny was continuously amazed when they went out, that Merle always bumped into people she knew. That did not change as the years went by. Merle still seemed to know everyone, people of all ages. Merle had more younger friends than anyone Fanny knew. And she had a great sense of humour, Fanny smiled to herself, thinking of the innumerable times they had laughed together. Merle knew how to use her sense of humour too, Fanny thought, to deflect any stress in life. She was very astute, and that sense of humour helped not only her, but her many friends as well, who were encouraged to substitute tears for laughter. Merle was aware that Fanny thought this about her, and for her part, she treasured Fanny as her friend who always put things together, was interested in everything around her and lived her long life extremely well. Merle hoped it was far from over.

Fanny thought a short visit to Merle's home would be just the ticket.

"COMING, COMING," FANNY heard from the other side of the door after she had knocked.

She would have just walked in, but the door was locked for some reason.

"Oh, Fanny, how good to see you." Merle grinned. "We were just about to call you to ask you to pop over."

"We?" Fanny looked into the kitchen, where she saw two younger women sitting at the table, tea cups in hand, both smiling warmly at her. "Oh, Noreen, Claire, hello. How are you both? I haven't seen you for a while."

Merle had met Claire at a scientific conference almost twenty years previously and the two had become friends. In time, their best friends, Fanny and Noreen, also met and the four women occasionally got together. They liked the perspective each brought—Fanny and Merle being older and Claire and Noreen being younger suited them all.

Merle put a cup in front of Fanny and poured some tea into it.

"We were just talking about what's happening at the university, in the Science department," Merle explained. "Noreen, why don't you tell Fanny what you were telling me."

Noreen turned in her chair and smiled at Fanny. Her red hair just touched the top of her plaid shirt. Her freckled face always made Fanny smile. Fanny thought she looked very colourful today.

"Well." Noreen sighed deeply and took a sip of her tea. "As you know, Claire and I are geneticists." Claire nodded at Fanny. "I'm sure since you used to be associated with the university, you know how hard it is to get funding for research. I know you're not a scientist but you're good friends with scientists, right?"

Fanny smiled at Noreen. She did enjoy these two. "No. No science for me. I always leave that up to Merle. I studied English and philosophy and worked in the library for years."

"And did very well there, I know. Well, let me tell you about our problem."

Fanny settled in, leaning back in the cushioned kitchen chair. She sipped her tea. She always looked forward to a good story and Noreen did not disappoint her.

Noreen told Fanny about Clovis and the research grants.

"Tell her about the ceiling," Claire urged.

"Ah yes, the ceiling." Noreen related the events of two weeks ago.

"A reinforced ceiling," murmured Fanny. "In a university. My goodness."

"You know, we asked him what his project was and were told it was confidential," Claire added.

"Confidential. Oh my." Now Fanny knew this would be interesting. "At a university? Where everyone is supposed to be open and accountable?"

"Yes, exactly." Noreen's freckles seemed to scrinch up under her eyes. Fanny always liked how that looked.

"We have no idea what's going on," Claire sadly stated. She moved her teaspoon so that it was precisely perpendicular to her teacup.

"I assume you've asked him," Fanny asked, tilting her head in a question.

"Sure. We ask him all the time," Noreen answered. "His responses are always very convoluted, and he has never specifically told us what he's up to or what he's working on. He has four other people in his lab with him, and they're all the same. Sworn to secrecy, they say. Secrecy from whom? Why? In science, sharing is so important. What could he be doing there that's taking our space and money?"

"And so," Merle said, "the girls came by to pick my brain, and now yours too, Fanny, to see what we can come up with and figure out what is going on."

"Sounds interesting. I'll help in any way I can." Fanny smiled at them.

Two hours passed quickly as they talked through the situation and tried to develop a plan of action. "How are you going to get into Clovis' lab?" Fanny asked, feeling like a secret agent.

After talking about several ideas that just wouldn't seem to work, Claire mentioned that she might be able to find someone who could help them. Patty had told her about someone who might be able to get into the lab. She went off to make a few telephone calls.

Claire returned fifteen minutes later. "Okay, I'm meeting this woman later today. I just told her we needed to talk with her. I'm hoping she'll help us when she hears the story."

"Okay, so we're decided then." Noreen put her hands on the kitchen table and pushed herself to a standing position. She arched her back in a long stretch. "With the help of Claire's friend, we break into the lab late Saturday night, when the place is deserted."

"She's not my friend. She's only someone Patty told me about. I've never actually met her."

"Okay, with the help of your not-friend. I sure hope this will work."

"Well," said Fanny, "you know what Nellie McClung said, don't you? 'Never apologize, never retreat, never explain. Get the thing done and let them howl.' And that's exactly what we'll do, right? Get the thing done, with Nellie McClung watching over our shoulders."

They all nodded and smiled. Fanny always seemed to come up with pithy remarks.

"You're right." Noreen smiled. "And you and Merle can come along as lookouts."

"BUNJIE, YOU WON'T believe what I'm doing this weekend!" Fanny exclaimed excitedly. She removed her hat and after carefully putting it away, hung up her coat, all the while telling the little bird what had happened that morning.

EVERYONE IN THE city knew that it was the STALAG women shooting at the men during the March. The March with its tragic events was the singular topic of conversation no matter who got together, no matter where they met. Claire was a little nervous about meeting Jo-Jo, one of the STALAG women, and was very relieved that Patty had agreed to come along. Patty had already told her about STALAG and the two different names of the group: the Serious Thelma and Louise Action Group and the Serious Thelma and Louise Army with Guns. After what happened at the March, Claire thought the second version was much more appropriate.

"I guess I have a right to be nervous," she mused.

Patty was much more in touch with the whole grass roots movement, Claire reflected, and was extremely friendly when meeting others. I don't mind meeting people, but I like working in the lab better. Science is precise. People aren't. I prefer precise.

The strong smell of the coffee jarred Claire out of her thoughts. She smiled up at Patty.

"Look, here she comes now." Patty set the cups down to go meet Jo-Jo.

Patty left Jo-Jo with Claire and went to get her coffee. Jo-Jo watched in fascination as Claire carefully folded her napkin into exact squares before speaking.

"So. What's up?" Jo-Jo asked.

Claire looked at the tall, thin woman wearing a black leather jacket and jeans, seated across from her. She had short, dark blonde hair. She looked at Jo-Jo's hands, with long, thin fingers, very strong looking. Something about her inspired confidence.

Claire held her cup between her hands, blew the steam away, and took a sip of her coffee. She put the cup down and wiped her lips with her very square napkin. She told Jo-Jo about the grant monies, the secret locked lab, and the Sertoli cells, the virus, and the fact that it could potentially kill all women.

Jo-Jo raised her eyebrows. "And I fit in . . . how?"

"Well," Claire said, placing her cup meticulously in the centre of her napkin, "we heard you were something of an expert in getting into places."

Jo-Jo smiled. "That I am."

"How d'you learn what to do?"

A big grin filled Jo-Jo's face. "My dad always wanted a boy, but he got me instead. He wanted to pass on all his knowledge, so he taught me everything he knew about breaking and entering and such things. He was incredibly good at it." She took a long sip of coffee. "But not quite good enough, because he's locked up now for the next fifteen years."

"Oh, I'm sorry to hear that," Patty commiserated.

"Yeah, well . . . what d'you want me to do?"

"We want you to help us break into Clovis' lab." Claire told Jo-Jo about the ceiling, the security. "It's not going to be easy."

"Well, I like a good challenge." Jo-Jo smiled. "All in the name of sisterhood, right?"

"Right," Patty echoed.

"You're new to Calgary, aren't you?" Claire asked.

"Yes, I am. Relatively new. I arrived here the last weekend of Stampede. Y'know, I thought the whole city had gone insane. I couldn't believe it. People dressing like cowboys, going to work like that, drinking, carrying on in the evenings. I had no idea. I thought I was in the wild west."

"Yeah, well, we do go a bit Western during Stampede." Patty smiled. "I like it."

"I loved it," Jo-Jo said. "I can hardly wait until next July, now that I know what to wear. I'm so anxious to go cowboy clothes shopping."

Claire and Patty laughed.

"Well, if you stay here for years, you'll certainly use your western wear," Patty said. "We go all out, every year."

"I gather most Calgarians do," Jo-Jo responded.

"And so we do. And so we do. Do you have your white cowboy hat yet?"

"No, not yet. Can't decide if I want a white one or a black one."

"Oh, you wanna be a bad guy, do you?" Patty teased.

They all laughed.

The topic of the March came up, as it did in most conversations in Calgary that year. Claire and Patty were interested in STALAG's participation.

"We decided to be very careful," Jo-Jo explained. "We were only going to use our guns if a woman, any woman, was actually injured by a man, and we were never going to do anything other than injure men to stop them from hurting women. We were all very clear about that. No killing. The group was devastated, as everyone is, I suppose, that three women were killed by the men. Some of our group were sorry we didn't retaliate in kind, but I still think we did the right thing."

They finished their coffee as they talked about the March, the university, and how women always seemed to get the worst end of things. They arranged to meet outside the Science Building on Saturday at ten p.m.

Jo-Jo mentioned that Claire might notice her there before

Saturday, casing the joint, she said, but if Claire did see her, she was to act as if she didn't know her.

Claire nodded and wondered with great perturbation of mind, what she was getting herself, and her friends, into.

NOVEMBER 21, 1992

One week later

FANNY WOKE UP very excited.

"It's Saturday, Bunjie," she told the little bird. "And you know what that means. I'm going to be a lookout."

In truth, Fanny didn't really know what a lookout actually did. "How difficult could it be?" she asked the little bird.

"I think I'll take a walk." She turned to her avian friend. "Just to clear my head, you know."

"Chirrup, chirp," Bunjie replied.

Fanny put on her coat, her mauve felt hat with the little feather on it, grabbed her purple purse, and walked out the door.

"Good-bye Bunjie, see you soon," she called over her shoulder.

"Chirpity, chirp" Bunjie replied.

Fanny started down the street. She loved her walks, loved them more all the time. One of the reasons was that she noticed as she got older, she became more and more invisible. She could watch people and the world happening around her with impunity; no one noticed an old woman these days. And Fanny loved watching people and the world happening around her.

Another reason she loved her walks so much was they gave her an opportunity to think without interruption. She didn't have to do anything except keep her feet moving, or sit on a bus bench or a rock. For someone approaching eighty years, Fanny was in such excellent shape, she could walk for many hours.

Fanny thought about the meeting last week at Merle's with Noreen and Claire. She was proud that they valued her opinion and was looking forward to being a spy, although Merle kept reminding her they were lookouts. Fanny knew they were really spies. She smiled in anticipation.

Then Fanny remembered being at the university library last week when she went to return her books and pick up some new ones.

There seemed to be an altercation at the desk between two men and the woman who worked there. Fanny couldn't help but overhear that the men were looking for documents; the librarian insisted they weren't there and the men insisted they were. They needed the documents for their research and according to them, they needed them now. If there was one thing Fanny knew well, it was libraries. She had worked almost half a century at this very library, ending up as director of the whole shebang.

She walked over to the desk and quietly said, "Pardon me for interrupting. I couldn't help but overhear. I do believe I can solve your problem."

Both men just shook their heads, ignored her completely, and went on arguing.

The librarian said, "Thank you madam, but this is a very complicated problem." And she turned back to the men.

Fanny just went up to the nearest computer, and within a few minutes, solved their problem. She showed it to the three of them. She remembered the look on the men's faces. They looked puzzled, then confused when she provided them with the information they needed. One man tipped his head to the side, his brow furrowed while he stared at her. She almost could hear his head whirring. "B-b-but that's an old lady. How can an old lady be so smart? How can an old lady know so many things?"

Out on the street, Fanny almost laughed out loud and put her hand up to her mouth.

And then her own head kicked in. "Fanny, shame on you. There's nothing wrong with laughing while walking in the street." She smiled as she turned the corner, going to her favourite park where she could sit on a large boulder, enjoy the blue sky, and watch the world go by.

Fanny made up stories about all the people she saw. She loved to play this game because that way, she could also make up all the endings. Mostly the happy endings went to the underdogs, as Fanny called them. The women, the marginalized children, the down and out men. They all had endings where they overcame life's oppressions and triumphed using their own brains. Granted, Fanny thought, sometimes people weren't overly endowed in the brain department, but nevertheless, she could give them a few extra grey cells in her fantasies. After all, they were her fantasies.

Fanny walked up the gravel path to her favourite boulder. It was large and perfect, almost like a rock chair, and she fit into it snuggly without having to climb very high at all. She sat, took a deep breath, and reached into her pocket pulling out a peach.

Fanny loved peaches. She loved them so much that when she was a child, three quarters of a century ago, she calculated, she was nicknamed "Peaches" because of her love of the fruit. She loved not only the taste, but the feel, the fuzziness of it all.

Fanny took a large bite and felt the juice run down her chin. She wiped at it with the napkin she had brought.

Hmm, she thought, just a bit over-ripe, but very good nevertheless.

Fanny sat there under the cloudless blue sky of the cool November day and thought about the past year; the past few years in fact. What a time it's been. Anyone who thought life slowed down when people aged were just wrong. This would be an exciting time, and not without a little danger either. She giggled, thinking of her spy days, which would begin that evening. Fanny knew that these women valued her presence in their group. Not like most of the world, who saw just an old woman.

She remembered when she had seen that cardiologist. He talked to her as though she were a total idiot, not answering any of her questions. Most people talked slower to her than they did to younger folks, and they certainly talked louder. Fanny didn't even need hearing aids, unlike most of her friends. She heard just fine, thank you. But most people could not seem to appreciate that. They seemed to think that as one aged, the IQ diminished along with the hearing.

Fanny took the last bite of the peach and sucked on the stone until there was no peach left at all. She then wrapped the stone in her napkin, wiped her juicy face and fingers, and put the napkin in her pocket so she could later drop it in the trash can on her way out of the park.

Yes, Fanny thought, smiling, for an old woman, it's still quite a life. And the most exciting part is only just beginning. And with that thought, she pushed herself off the rock and slowly walked back home to Bunjie.

FANNY AND MERLE arranged to drive to the university together. Merle pulled up in front of Fanny's building and Fanny eagerly slid into the front seat. They looked at each other and burst out laughing.

"I know this is serious, and what we are doing is illegal and possibly dangerous, but I can't help it." Merle collapsed, laughing, over the steering wheel.

"I know, it's exciting, isn't it?" chortled Fanny. "But we had best get the giggles out of the way before we get to the university."

They both tried very hard, mostly unsuccessfully, to look serious.

"LOOK WHO'S HERE," Noreen called out to Claire as she entered the lab followed by the two older women she had just met outside the building.

"Shush, someone will hear you," Claire whispered loudly.

"Oh, for heaven's sakes, we both checked the whole building and no one is here except Leo. He's downstairs watching TV. Who's going to hear me except us?"

"Well, we still have to be careful." Claire lined her pencil up precisely even with the edge of her desk.

"Look," Noreen said, in a quieter voice, "isn't it time to meet this Jo-Jo? Do you want to bring her up here?"

"Okay." Claire stood up and pushed her chair neatly against the desk. "I'll go down to get her." She silently closed the door behind her.

Fanny, Merle, and Noreen all smiled at each other, the odd giggle escaping, all eager for the events of the evening to unfurl. Fanny did like looking at Noreen's freckles, especially when she laughed.

THE INTRODUCTIONS MADE, everyone focused on Jo-Jo.

"Okay, I checked this place out earlier this week," Jo-Jo said. "That lab is alarmed, so the very first thing we have to do is disable the alarm."

"I never thought of that," Merle muttered. "We never had alarms in my day."

"Well, we most definitely have them now." Jo-Jo moved toward the door. "And I'm pretty sure after hearing what Claire told me," she turned to smile at Claire, "that they have more than a simple lock on that lab."

"Okay, so whadda we do first?" Noreen leaned against her desk.

"First, we go down to the basement to turn off the alarm," Jo-Jo said.

"The basement? But no—Leo's there," Claire burst out.

"Leo?" Merle raised her eyebrows.

"The security guard."

"Oh, I know that." Jo-Jo smiled. "I've done my homework. We're going to sneak by him. I only need one more person to come with me."

"I'll go." Noreen anxiously jumped up.

"Okay. You three wait here," Jo-Jo put her hand on the doorknob, "and Noreen and I will be back in a few minutes. But after that, we will have to work very quickly."

JO-JO AND NOREEN took the stairs to the basement. They heard Leo's TV blaring from the lounge.

Jo-Jo peeked into the room and whispered, "He's fallen asleep. Come."

They quickly walked down the concrete-walled hall, past the storage rooms, and entered an electrical room, which had the fuse boxes and alarms for the building.

"Here they are. This is the one we want," Jo-Jo whispered. "You keep looking down that hall and let me know if there is any movement."

Jo-Jo took a little tool kit out of the pocket of her leather jacket and very gingerly detached wires. She carefully labeled them.

"Okay, we're all set. Let's do this."

They crept by sleeping Leo again and quietly ran up the stairs.

Once they were all outside of Clovis' lab, Jo-Jo addressed the eldest two. "Okay, one of you down this hall, one of you down there. If you see or hear anything other than us, rap loudly on the wall. Got it?"

Merle and Fanny took their positions. They could see one another but were too far apart to talk without shouting. Fanny adjusted her hat, the one that the saleswoman at the hat boutique had told her was Delicious Plum. Fanny wished it could have been Delicious Peach instead, but then the hat would have been a pinky/orange. She liked the purple, rather Delicious Plum, a lot. And she loved the wide brim which she thought was very spy-like. She looked around surreptitiously, paced a few steps, and whispered to herself, "I'm a spy!" She could hardly wait to tell Bunjie.

In the meantime, Jo-Jo had her little kit out and was working on the lock to Clovis' lab. Claire and Noreen stood anxiously behind her, notebooks and pens in hand. They had already decided that even if there was a copier in the lab, they didn't want to risk using it. They wanted it to appear as though no one had come at all, and agreed they were going to be very careful about moving things.

In less than a minute, Jo-Jo whispered, "Okay, we're in," and she opened the outer door. Claire and Noreen walked very quickly into the room and fidgeted anxiously while Jo-Jo worked on the inner door. In what seemed like seconds, she held it open for them. They all walked inside, Noreen turning to the right, Claire to the left, while Jo-Jo stood at the door.

Fanny was already getting a little bored. She leaned against the wall and pulled down her hat. She noticed a chair through the door of a room across the hall. She walked over, pulled the chair just outside the door, ever so quietly, and sat down. She waved at Merle, who waved back.

Inside Clovis' lab, Noreen and Claire were looking and writing. Claire saw a computer and quickly scanned through files, taking notes as she scrolled. Noreen checked all the desks and contents of their drawers, full of handwritten notes, reports from experiments, and a few papers with handwriting she couldn't read.

After twenty-five minutes Jo-Jo whispered, "Okay, times up. Lco will be here soon on his rounds. Best finish up."

"Oh, but there's more." Claire reluctantly left the computer.

"C'mon, Claire, I think we have enough now," Noreen whispered. "Let's be smart about this."

The three walked out of the lab and Jo-Jo rapidly relocked the door. They got Fanny and Merle and went back to their own lab where the lights were on. Fanny, Merle, and Jo-Jo went into the inner room, and sat quietly in the dark.

NOT FIVE MINUTES later, Leo opened the door.

"Oh, hi. What are you two doing here on a Saturday night?"

"Hi, Leo." Noreen casually leaned against her desk. "We had this great idea so came down here to write our notes. We won't be much longer."

"Okay, it's your life." Leo smiled, shaking his black curly-haired head. He closed the door behind him and continued on his rounds.

Jo-Jo quickly came from the inner room, looked down the hall, and dashed to the basement to reconnect the alarm. The others anxiously waited for her return. Once she was back, they turned off the lights, locked the doors, and left the building.

"Can we give you a ride somewhere, Jo-Jo?" Claire asked.

"Sure. I left my car outside the university. I'll show you. But I'd sure like to know what you found."

"Of course. We're all going to our house for a debriefing," Noreen said. "You're more than welcome to join us." She looked grim and pale as she got into the car.

THE WARM, HOMEY smell of the cedar log burning in the fireplace was discordant with the anxious pacing of Denise and Patty, who were waiting for the others to return.

"Well?" Denise cocked her head at Noreen as soon as she opened the door.

"Just give me a minute, hon. By the way, this is Jo-Jo."

"Hi, Jo-Jo. Welcome. Hi, Fanny, Merle. Come on in. What can I get you all to drink?"

Once they were all settled with drinks and seated in front of the fireplace, Denise turned again to Noreen. "So?"

Noreen and Claire sat on one sofa, their hands full of notes, facing the other five who watched them anxiously. Noreen looked stricken. Claire was clearly unhappy. They shuffled their papers and looked at each other.

"C'mon," urged Patty. "Spill, already."

"Well," began Claire, "we talked about this on the way back in the car. We found notes about the virus, the one which attacks the Sertoli cells."

"Oh, is that the one that kills men?" Patty wriggled on the soft burnt orange chair, trying to get even more comfortable.

"We can't say that for sure," Claire continued. "We only know that there is evidence of a virus that damages the Y chromosome."

"But that's the chromosome that determines a male human," Merle offered.

"Yep, that's right," Noreen said. "We're not sure why they're working with this virus. We found something else that we're not sure how to interpret."

"What's that?" asked Jo-Jo, leaning forward, elbows on her knees.

"Well, it looks like when they were working with the initial virus that destroyed the Sertoli cells, they found an antidote, so to speak. We think it might allow them to differentiate so only males are born."

"Why would they want to do that?" asked Fanny.

"Again, not sure," said Noreen, "but we found something even more alarming."

"What?" Merle adjusted a gold plush pillow behind her back.

"It looks as though the government is very much involved in all this," Claire continued. "On the computer, I found letters from some minister in the government, and they were marked 'top secret.'"

"Wow." Jo-Jo shook her head. "This is big."

"Yes, it is," Noreen agreed. "Very big."

DECEMBER 9, 1992

Two and a half weeks later

GENERAL SONDERMAN WAS happy. He had done the right thing. "I always do the right thing." He smiled to himself. From the day that kid West, who worked as a researcher at the university science labs, told his uncle about his work, the General was ready. It was more than good luck that West's uncle happened to be the assistant to the General and was stationed outside this very door. As soon as he began talking about the work West and his lab-mates were doing, and more importantly, what they could be doing, General Sonderman knew that he had found what he was looking for. He couldn't have imagined a better scenario. One meeting with the Head of the Science Department, a meeting with that Dr. Clovis, and he was on his way.

DR. CLEVE CLOVIS walked down the hallway, adjusting his suit jacket and straightening his tie. In front of the door with the name General Steven Sonderman etched into the glass, he stopped, ran a hand through his wavy brown hair, straightened his glasses, and rapped on the door.

"Come in," a voice bellowed from inside the room.

He shut the door quietly behind him and sat down across the desk from General Sonderman.

The General was a large man, six feet four, solidly built, very fit, with very short, greying hair. His uniform was simple, yet somehow elegant.

"Come in, come in, Doctor," he boomed. "Sit."

Dr. Clovis already had, so he smiled uncomfortably back at the General and shrugged.

"So. How's our little project coming along?" asked the General.

"Pretty good. Pretty good," Clovis replied. "As you know, we discovered this virus that had the potential to harm living males."

"I understood it discovered you." The General smiled. "It was a mistake, right? But do go on."

Clovis smiled back weakly. "Uh, yes, well, we wanted to try to find something to counteract it. So we discovered something else."

"Again," the General interrupted, "it found you. It was another accident, I understand."

"No matter." Clovis cleared his throat. "The point is, that we can now, at will, produce only male humans. And now we are working on how to fine tune those males."

"By making them good and strong, for our new armies, yes?"

"That's the gist of it, sir."

"And when we get our armies of men, we can take the first virus which you still have, and use it on our enemies to wipe out their males, right?"

"Yes, sir, that's the thinking, I suppose."

"You suppose right, Doctor. I think in the future, we will only meet here. I won't come to your workplace again, nor will anyone from my staff or the government. This project has become top secret and we don't want anyone not involved suspecting anything. What about the other scientists at your workplace? What do they know about your work?"

"They know nothing, sir. Nothing. On my floor are just two girls working in genetics and two other labs run by post-docs working on immunological problems. I've instructed security never to allow anyone into the lab who isn't authorized, at any time. There is some curiosity about that, but it will pass. Each scientist is concerned with his own problems, not mine."

"Good, good. And what about the people who work in your lab?"

"We've had long talks as you suggested, General. I think I made it very clear to all of them that it's in their best interests not to talk to anyone about our work. If you know what I mean." Clovis grinned.

"Good. Good. The government representative will be very happy to hear all this. Keep up the good work, Clovis. I'll contact you when to meet again. Unless of course, another virus discovers you, heh, heh, heh." He chortled.

Clovis swallowed uncomfortably. "Yes, sir. Thank you, General." He got up to walk to the door.

"Doctor, good work. You are helping me and the country. No doubt one day you'll be famous. We'll be in touch."

Clovis walked out the door and closed it softly behind him. Alone in the hallway, he grinned broadly. "Famous, eh? That'll show those two stupid broads. Famous . . ." He grinned as he walked out the building, dreaming of how respectfully he would be treated by others once he was famous.

DECEMBER 14, 1992

Five days later

CLAIRE ALWAYS LIKED Monday mornings. She enjoyed her weekends, but Monday mornings back at work often meant starting something new or continuing with a project she enjoyed. She truly loved her work, and according to Patty, maybe a little too much. She sat at her desk with a folder of papers in hand, happily planning the work for the coming week.

"Mornin'." Noreen breezed into the room. "How are things with you this morning?"

"Oh, pretty good. Thinking a lot. You know, about our problem down the hall."

"I do know. I've been thinking about it all weekend too." Noreen plopped her briefcase and purse down on her desk.

"You know what really bothers me, almost most of all?" Noreen settled in her chair. "What bothers me is this government involvement. How can that be? What do they want? Why is it so secret?"

"So are we going to do anything?" Claire ventured.

"Sure," answered Noreen. "But exactly what, I have no idea. Any thoughts?"

Throughout the day, they tried to do their work but kept coming back to the problem of Dr. Cleve Clovis and his lab.

DECEMBER 23, 1992

One week later

WHEN JO-JO WAS asked by Patty and Claire to meet with them, she looked forward to the possibility of potential new friends. The women she knew from STALAG were okay, but Jo-Jo, new to Calgary, was anxious to get acquainted with others. She liked both Patty and Claire, and was very interested in the whole genetics thing regarding those Sertoli cells and men. She hoped she could somehow be involved in finding out what was really going on in that lab. She was thrilled when Noreen and Denise invited her to their home for a dinner party, a small holiday gathering, they said.

Jo-Jo had come to Calgary to see her mother, Marcy, who recently moved back to the city after an absence of almost fifty years. Marcy had been born in Calgary and lived the first six years of her life there, but was moved to New York where eventually Jo-Jo was born and grew up. Jo-Jo had never been enamoured with New York, although she thrived there, and had many friends.

She told Marcy she had been thinking recently of leaving New York and changing her life. Jo-Jo thought of Marcy not only as her mother but as her best friend. They told each other everything.

"I was associated too much with dad in New York," she explained to Marcy, who had left her husband a decade ago.

"I mean, I'm glad he taught me so much, I really am, but I wish he would've taught me more things that were, well . . . legal, I guess. I'm getting a bit tired of always having to outwit the cops, although I must admit that at times, it's fun to always be a few steps ahead."

Marcy laughed sympathetically. She always felt a certain amount of guilt that she had given Jo-Jo a father like Rex, who was so well-known by the police. And that Jo-Jo had chosen to stay in New York rather than go away with her when she left. Rex had been a good husband, was a wonderful man, she had to admit, kind and funny and sensitive, but she could no longer live with his illegal activities.

"Well, you know, whatever you decide, I'll support you." She put an arm around Jo-Jo.

"I dunno, Mom, I came here to see you and be part of STALAG. I got involved with them in New York, y'know, but I never was very keen to be packing."

Marcy nodded gratefully.

"After that March, I'm even less keen. Three women murdered. Three. And seven guys injured. That whole scene totally freaked me out. I almost thought seriously about going right back to New York, where three dead is no biggie, y'know? But here it is."

Jo-Jo told Marcy about the new women she met and how they had first contacted her for a B & E.

"But I really like them and they keep inviting me to their homes. They are so smart. Two of them are genetics scientists who work at the University. One is a therapist—I really like her, Denise. She's always so calm. And Patty, she's super cool—an artist. And they have two old lady friends - even in NYC, I never met women like these two. Very wonderful women. So who knows? Maybe I can be part of a group that doesn't always break the law."

JO-JO HAD FALLEN in love with Calgary and since she had been planning to leave New York City anyway, decided to stay. There was something about the fresh air, the mountains, the fact that Calgary was tiny compared to New York, yet it was a real city with good restaurants, and interesting theatre, which she loved. And some strong feminists. Really, she had everything she needed and staying with her mom until she could get her own home had been wonderful; the two remained close and spoke daily. Jo-Jo had been devastated when Marcy disclosed that she had cancer, but she seemed to be doing okay with the treatments, and they were both hopeful for a total recovery. Jo-Jo looked forward to the time when Marcy could come with her to the mountains, which she went to as often as possible.

Jo-Jo loved her new apartment overlooking the Bow River. She could walk along the path beside the river for miles. She could sit inside, curled up in her window seat, and look out at the water and watch the people. But the most amazing thing, she thought, was the quiet. She didn't hear horns honking and people yelling twenty-four hours a day. It was peaceful and she was grateful for the silence.

JANUARY 5, 1993

Two weeks later

"DR. CLEVE CLOVIS, will you please come up to the podium."

Cleve Clovis stood up, swiped a hand over his wavy brown hair, straightened his glasses, smiled, and walked up to the stage.

"Dr. Cleve Clovis, on behalf of the Scientific Community of Canada, we wish to honour you here tonight and to present you with this small token of our appreciation for the work you have done."

The burst of applause felt very good. The award, Clovis thought, looked remarkably like an Oscar. Still smiling, holding the Oscar-like award, Clovis stood on the stage while the large audience got to their feet, still applauding. He could see many of the people he worked with in the audience, and there, in the front row, off to the side, were Noreen Stanton and Claire Christopher, clapping and cheering along with the others. Clovis felt wonderful. He was very pleased within himself.

He heard a noise above the clapping, and looked to both sides of the stage and out into the audience, but could not detect where it was coming from. It was a buzzing that sounded very like an alarm clock.

With a sinking feeling, he realized it was indeed his alarm clock, and lay in his bed devastated that he was interrupted in his dream.

At least, he thought, I could have had the damn dream earlier so I could have dreamt more of it.

He did not feel like getting out of bed after he turned the alarm off. He decided to stay in bed another few minutes and skip his breakfast and newspaper. He could always have coffee at work. Clovis thought about the actual time he attended the awards presentation. That night, the award for outstanding work in the scientific community went to Stanton and Christopher, his nemesis. He often thought of them as one unit. They were in graduate school together, got their PhDs the same year, and currently worked together. And the two of them had always taken away any recognition he should get. He remembered in graduate school they were friendly enough, but anyone could be friendly if they were always considered the best. And they always were.

Clovis sat up in bed and swung his feet onto the mat on the floor. He stood up, stretching his arms high over his head.

"One day," he told himself, "I am going to get an award. A big award. And I will become famous and those two will have to kowtow to me. Everyone will, but especially those two girls. Once I am famous, everyone will know I am a good scientist. A good person. Soon this will happen," he assured his mirror self. "Soon."

JANUARY 7, 1993

Two days later

RIGHT AFTER THE Christmas holidays, Fanny and Merle had decided to call all the women together to talk. After all, Fanny reminded Merle, they had been spies.

"Lookouts," Merle corrected.

"Yes," said Fanny, "spies."

They still felt very involved in and curious about this Clovis thing. Merle made some phone calls and by the next night, the women met at Merle's house. Noreen and Denny arrived first, then Claire and Patty, with Jo-Jo in tow. Merle had asked Patty to bring Jo-Jo, wondering if they might not need her skills again. Jo-Jo was delighted to be included.

They talked late into the evening about how to deal with what they now called The Clovis Problem and his work with The Y Syndrome. They thought saying the sperm in his lab all had The Y Syndrome was quite humorous. Before they disbanded, they decided that they would try to follow Clovis when he left the building, to see where he went and what he did. Jo-Jo volunteered to do this. Her dad taught her well, not only about B & E but other handy skills, such as how to follow someone undetected. The women agreed to meet again in a few weeks, hear from Jo-Jo on Clovis' activities, and discuss what else to do.

JANUARY 20, 1993

Two weeks later

JO-JO SAT IN her car, drinking a coffee. She kept her eyes on Clovis' Caddy which was parked adjacent to the Science Building. She could see the front door of the building and knew he was in his lab. She had been tailing him now for twelve days. Nothing of interest was happening, at least of interest to her or the other women. Denise's words kept echoing in her head.

"Look," Denise reasoned, "let's do a little reality check here. This is Canada. We don't shoot people here. The March violence was an aberration. The army doesn't have secret plans. The government doesn't have secret plans. We had better be damned sure that we are dealing with something that concerns us and other people. Things here just don't add up for me."

On some level, Jo-Jo agreed with her. Things in fact did not add up. Even Clovis, whom she thought was quite a boring man, appeared to be anything but dangerous. Jo-Jo had no trouble confirming this by tailing him. He worked at the lab, always had lunch at the faculty club, always ate the same thing in fact: chicken sandwich on rye, salad, and coffee. He usually sat alone at a small table in the corner. He left work at five p.m. every day, unusual for a scientist, and drove straight home. He lived in a modest house on the outskirts of Mount Royal. Apparently his wife left him several years ago. He now lived alone. He ate dinner around six-thirty, watched TV for a few hours, and then he went to bed. She had even found out his favourite TV shows were *MASH* and *Columbo*. He was definitely a man with a routine and very prosaic tastes. Jo-Jo thought this a sad sort of existence, and almost felt sorry for him, until she remembered what he was doing in his lab. If in fact, he really was doing what Claire and Noreen said.

NEAR THE END of the second week, finally something interesting happened. Just before two p.m. on a Wednesday afternoon, Clovis left the Science Building, got into his car, and drove off. Jo-Jo was not far behind.

She watched him drive into the army base off Sarcee Trail. Jo-Jo parked her car outside the base and walked in, telling the sentry she was meeting a friend for a drink. She walked down the narrow roadway surrounded by wooden one-story buildings that looked remarkably alike, until she located Clovis' car parked in a lot outside a green graceless structure in the middle of the compound. She very innocently opened the door to the building and entered a long corridor lined with office doors. On the doors were the names: General Marvin Wellington, General John Cassidy, General Steven Sonderman, General Leo Mariner. Four Generals, Jo-Jo though. Wow. Why do we need four Generals? The other offices seemed to be administrative offices; she could hear the clickety-clack of keyboards, the occasional ring of a telephone.

"Can I help you?"

Jo-Jo whirled around to see a young man in uniform.

"Uh, no, thank you. I'm meeting a friend for a drink and must have walked into the wrong building. Sorry."

"Do you know which building you want?"

"Yes, that one over there. I'll go over there now."

"Okay," said the soldier, sounding like he didn't quite believe her.

Jo-Jo walked around the building and looked through the back door window, just in time to see a door open and Clovis walk into the hall. She waited until the soldier guarding the hallway turned a corner and quickly ran in to look at the name on the door. General Steven Sonderman.

"Well, well," she muttered, "what is a dork like Clovis doing with a General? What is going on here?"

She rushed back to the parking lot in time to see Clovis' car pull out and drive off. She drove quickly to get back to the university before he did and watched him pull into his parking space and walk back into the Science Building. He seemed to have a bounce in his step. He definitely had a smile on his face.

"This does not bode well," she said.

JANUARY 23, 1993

Three days later

THE WOMEN HAD decided that whatever was going on in Clovis' lab was seriously important, and that they should now get together often to share information. Jo-Jo was tailing Clovis; Noreen and Claire were watching the lab and listening for any talk at work that might be relevant; Patty and Denny were keeping tabs in the women's community in case there was talk or action that might be helpful; Merle and Fanny—they were organizing the meetings.

They gathered at Noreen's and Denny's house.

"I have good news and bad news." Noreen began the meeting.

"Let's hear them both," said Patty. "Good news first. Then the bad news won't seem so bad."

"Okay. The good news is this. There's this woman, Joanie, who works in Clovis' lab. I've known her for probably fifteen years. She's a nice enough woman. She couldn't find a job anywhere else so took the position with Clovis but I know she doesn't like it. So yesterday I had coffee with her. Secretly. And what she told me is the bad news."

"Do tell." Patty fidgeted in anticipation.

Noreen sat back and remembered yesterday's meeting with Joanie. She had bumped into Joanie in the hall earlier that week and casually mentioned they should get together for coffee one day. To her surprise, Joanie seemed quite agreeable to this suggestion and they picked a time two days hence.

They met off campus as arranged, and Joanie immediately began, "I really shouldn't be meeting with you. I'm not supposed to be talking to other scientists."

"Oh, that's ridiculous. Who says so?"

"My boss says so, that's who. For the last four months, things have really changed. There are all kinds of rules now—no talking with other scientists, no talking to *anyone* about the work we do, things like that. Nori, it's terrible. We've been threatened with all kinds of things if we break the rules, and now the threats are getting scary. They've even threatened our families! I wanted to leave Clovis' lab, and was told that was out of the question. No one is allowed to leave. No one new is allowed to start work there. Everyone has their job to do, but we are not even allowed to share our work with other people in the same lab. How crazy is that? He has everyone and everything separated. I feel as though I'm going nuts. I have to talk to someone, even though I know it's a huge risk. You have to understand this can't get out or I could really suffer. And I'm scared for my family too."

"That's okay." Noreen encouraged her friend. "You can talk with me. We know there is something fishy going on there anyway. Maybe we can help you. You can help us. And we'll sort out this whole Clovis scene."

"So what *do* you know?" Joanie raised her eyebrows and looked straight at Noreen.

"Well, we think he's doing something with Sertoli cells but we're not sure exactly what."

"Well, hang onto your hat. Yes, we're working with Sertoli cells all right. We've been changing the environment within seminiferous tubules, so the Sertoli cells can't facilitate progression of germ cells to spermatozoa. So no production of sperm. Also we've been working with FGF9 which activates Sertoli cells. No FGF9 always causes a female to develop."

Nori grinned. "Well, isn't that a good thing?" she asked facetiously.

Joanie ignored the comment. "Clovis decided to try the reverse. He played with the genes and Sertoli cells and now can also cause only males to develop."

"Wow," Noreen said. "Claire and I think this work should be called The Y Syndrome.

Joanie smiled. "And get this. Somehow a university hotshot found out about this work and soon the government found out and now we think the army is involved."

"The army. What has the army got to do with Sertoli cells and sexual differentiations?"

"Think about it. If a government has the capacity to make all males, think how big the army can be—and any men who get killed can just be replaced. And if they can get the original virus, where just females are produced, into the enemy country, then they wouldn't have any men for their armies. Right now you can get the virus for this through an injection into the blood stream but Clovis is now working on an aerosol to disseminate it."

"Wait a minute," Noreen interrupted. "You mean you spray the stuff and no more men get born?"

"Yeah, that's right."

"Well, are the females who get born normal?"

"Presumably," answered Joanie. "Look, I think the whole thing is way over the top. Some of us have argued and argued with Clovis, but he is so thrilled that the government is now involved he won't hear any of it. He just tells us to get back to work and not make waves or else. And the 'or else' is not something anyone would want to experience."

Noreen shook her head, remembering she was back in her living room with all the others anxiously waiting for her to talk. After she told them the basics of what Joanie had told her, everyone started loudly discussing this new information at the same time.

"Wait a minute, wait a minute. Calm down. Let's not all talk at once. One at a time." Denise often adopted the role of peacemaker; her work as one of the best therapists in Calgary came in handy even in her own living room with her friends.

Each woman had a chance to vent her outrage. Then they started to plan.

"I think we should ask Joanie to join us," Patty said.

"We can't," answered Noreen. "She took a huge gamble meeting with me once. We'll have to figure out a way to support her as best we can until this whole thing is settled."

They talked well into the evening about what each one of them would do.

FEBRUARY 3, 1993

Eleven days later

PATTY SIPPED HER coffee as she sat in the passenger seat of Jo-Jo's old Chevy. She had decided to keep Jo-Jo company and besides, she wanted to be in on tailing the bad guy. Even though she knew the situation was serious and potentially dangerous, there was still an air of excitement about the whole thing, a real rush. She smiled.

Jo-Jo, both hands resting on the steering wheel, was looking straight ahead, deep in thought. They liked each other and were comfortable sitting together in silence.

"Oh look, here he comes, just like clockwork, every other Wednesday afternoon." Jo-Jo shifted in her seat, started the motor, and pulled out. She knew where Clovis was going. She drove to the army base, left her car outside the fence, and she and Patty demurely walked up to a sentry and stated they were coming to speak to the army wives and were expected. The sentry waved them in. They walked along the main road until they came to the low green building that housed the generals. Clovis' car was in the parking lot.

"I'm going around to the back of the building," Jo-Jo said. "You stay here and watch."

Jo-Jo went around the back and peered down the hall through the window. The soldier monitoring the building was nowhere to be seen.

Patty was curious. She wanted to see what was in that building that was so important. She walked up to the window in the front door, saw only an empty hallway, and quietly let herself in. She slowly walked down the hall, reading the names on the doors.

Wow, she thought, so many generals. How did Clovis ever get involved with this?

"Can I help you, ma'am?" she heard from directly behind her.

Patty twirled around to see a soldier standing very close to her.

"Who is it you are looking for?" he asked.

"Well, I'm uh, well, you see, er, I just wanted to see what was here," she blurted.

"And why is that?" asked the soldier.

"No reason." Patty looked down at her sneakers.

"Follow me please," the soldier instructed.

"Uh no, I can't, I mean I have a friend, I mean I have to meet someone out there . . ." She started to walk toward the door.

"Follow me please, ma'am." The soldier put his hand firmly around her arm and propelled her down the hall into a room with a long wooden table and several brown uncomfortable-looking chairs.

"Have a seat please, ma'am. Someone will be with you shortly."

"No, but I have to go, I have someone waiting for me, I was just looking. You can't keep me here . . ."

"Ma'am, please sit down and be quiet. Someone will be with you shortly." He walked out of the room, closed the door, and Patty heard the click of the lock.

She looked around the room—there were no windows. How could she tell Jo-Jo where she was? What was she going to do now? She jumped up to check the door. Surely that soldier wouldn't have locked her in there. She very quietly tried to turn the door handle. First to the right; then to the left. She tried to push it in, pull it out, and turned it again. She had to admit she was definitely locked in. She returned to her seat and wrung her hands.

Within a few minutes a tall, handsome man with very short grey hair walked in. He looked important, with all the medals on his uniform. And behind him was none other than Dr. Cleve Clovis.

"Do you know this one, doc?" the tall man asked.

"She looks familiar, General. She's not one of the scientists though. Oh, yeah. I remember who you are. You're Claire Christopher's friend. I remember you from staff parties. What's your name again?"

Patty remained silent.

"Young lady, answer the questions when they are asked," the General bellowed. He turned to Clovis, shaking his head. "These broads are all alike, aren't they?" There was something very sinister in his demeanour.

There was a loud knock on the door. The General opened it.

"General, come quickly," the soldier yelled. "The alarm went off in your office. We think there is an intruder there."

The men raced down the hall after locking Patty back in the room.

Within seconds Patty heard something at the door. The door swung open and Jo-Jo whispered, "Patty, hurry, follow me."

The two women ran down the hall, out the building, and off the army base.

"Phew, that was close." Jo-Jo sighed, once they were safe in the car and on their way back to the university. "What were you doing in that building?"

"I was just curious to see what was in there," Patty answered, somewhat contritely. "I'm sorry Jo-Jo. I didn't mean to cause trouble."

"No trouble. It all worked out okay. I'm just glad I saw where they were taking you. When I saw the general go into the room, it was easy to hot wire his alarm to get them out of that interrogation room."

"Interrogation room?" Patty gave her an alarmed look.

"Well, what did you expect? You were found basically trespassing on army property. Did you think they were going to hand you a bouquet of flowers?" Jo-Jo laughed. "Just be thankful it all worked out okay."

"ARE YOU *SURE* there's no leak in your lab?" the General asked Clovis.

"I have been very careful," Clovis responded. "I am sure there is no leak. I have no idea what that girl was doing here."

"Well, it looks as though there may have been more than one here. I just heard that the alarm in my office had been tampered with. Her accomplice probably did that to help her escape. I mean, she's just a girl, I doubt she could do any damage, but still . . . we now have to work quickly and be very careful."

"What should I be doing?"

"Well, first of all, I think we need to move everyone not associated with your team off that floor," the General said.

"Oh, General, that'll be difficult. There are a couple of scientists there, that girl's friend in fact is one of them, who are very well known and quite high up in the scientific hierarchy. They're not going to want to move."

"But they're going to have to," the General stated. "It's now a matter of government security. I'll talk to the university president and make sure that they are out of there as quickly as possible."

"They're not going to like that, sir."

"Do you really care what some broads like or don't like, doctor? We have a job to do and we're almost finished with it, right? Do you actually think the army and the government are going to let two girl scientists stand in our way? Don't be such a moron." General Sonderman stood up. "Don't let this incident today deter you. Keep up the good work. We'll take care of the rest. Soon you'll have that whole floor to yourself. Good day for now, doctor."

"Good day, General. Thank you sir."

Clovis walked out the door and sighed in relief. He realized the General had scared him and shook his head, thinking how frightening that man could be whenever he raised his voice.

CLOVIS DROVE BACK to the lab after the meeting, and then promptly at five, drove home. It wasn't until he was safely inside, that he took a deep breath and felt his body relax. He ached from being so stiff. He realized that the General had really unsettled him earlier. He had no idea why Claire Christopher's friend was at the army base that afternoon. It didn't make sense to him. But that wasn't his fault. He knew nothing about her. Why was the General so angry? He didn't do anything wrong.

For the first time in months, Clovis poured himself a drink before dinner. He smiled with the first sip, thinking he was such a Canadian drinking his CC and seven. He went out the back door and sat on the deck, again something he hadn't done for a long time. Although it was February, a Chinook wind blew all day, and it was unseasonably warm.

"I need to think," he said softly, but once he said that, he really didn't know what he wanted to think about. Things just kept swirling though his mind and he had trouble concentrating on just one thing.

How did I get like this? he asked himself. I wasn't always like this. I used to be a good man when Allie was here. I thought we were happy together. I should have spent more time at home with her though. She always said I worked too hard, spent too much time in the lab. Well, too bad she didn't stay. She would have ended up being the wife of a famous scientist.

Clovis grinned. He relaxed with the help of his alcohol. Well, okay, she's gone. Truth be told, he missed her a lot. He used to love coming home to his wife waiting there for him. When she left, she told him her life was amounting to nothing. All she did was keep house for him and he could hire someone to do that. He was very surprised at the time. He had been happy in his marriage and was shocked that she was not. When she moved out of the city to go back to her family, he kept the house. He was glad he did. He liked this house. He was secure and comfortable here.

"I should come outside onto the deck more often," Clovis said out loud. "It's a bit chilly now, but in the spring it will be nice. Maybe I'll hire a gardener this year, now that I have more money. I can put in some flowers. Once I'm famous, people will want to come over. It will have to look good." He finished his drink and went back into the house to see what he could make for dinner.

FEBRUARY 8, 1993

Five days later

"WHAT? THEY ARE moving us where? Who told you this? What the hell is going on around here?" Noreen stormed around her office, slamming down books and files and anything else she could find.

"I spoke with the university president for a long time, Nori. I even begged, but Weber said Clovis' work was confidential. I argued that this was a university and things should be out in the open. He agreed, but he said that the government had taken over this lab, and he really had no say. So we're being moved down to the main floor. There are some empty labs there we can use."

"I'm not going. I don't want to move," shouted Noreen.

"Sorry, Dr. Stanton." Leo walked into their room. "They called me in today and a couple of the other security guards from evening shift. We're here to help you relocate. I'm really sorry about this, but we have our orders."

"Orders. *Orders*! Who is giving you these orders?" screamed Noreen.

"Nori, calm down. There's nothing we can do about this now. Let's go down to the new labs, and we can talk about things there." Claire walked over to Noreen and put her hand on her shoulder.

Noreen shrugged her hand off and stomped out of the room. She turned her head and shouted, "If you wanna move me, then move me. I'm not helping *one bit*!" She slammed the door behind her.

FEBRUARY 13, 1993

Five days later

NOREEN SMASHED THE book down on the desk, scattering papers all over the floor.

"What's the matter? What're you doing?" Claire had just walked into their new first-floor office.

"I hate the whole fuckin' world, is what I'm doing," Noreen shouted and slammed the book down again on the desk.

"What's going on? Whatever are you on about?"

"It's not fair, it's just not fair."

"I know. It's not fair. What's not fair?"

"The whole thing. The whole fucking thing. First, he takes our money. *Our* money. Then he takes our lab. *Our* lab. And now—no one even knows what we're doing. And when we find what we're looking for, they probably won't even care, because he already took it all away from us." She swept three books off her desk onto the floor.

"Nori, stop. You're not even making sense. Look what you're doing to this office. Stop. Sit down. Let's talk about this."

"There's nothing to talk about, and you know it. You know there's nothing to say. He beat us. That fucking guy one-upped us. How is that even possible?"

"He didn't beat us or one-up us," Claire reassured her friend. "Our work is going well. So what, we have to work in this smaller lab. We're still working together, right? We're still discovering really important things, right? He can do whatever he wants, in as big a lab as he wants, but he's dumb. You know that. He doesn't know genetics like we do, he doesn't know much of anything. Why are you letting him get to you?"

"Because he fuckin' *beat* us, that's why."

"He didn't beat us, because he can't beat us. We're women and he is only a man. We're smarter, better. He can't beat us in anything.

And you know that. So stop acting like a spoiled child and come back to work. You're a woman, not a man—you can do anything you want. Come with me. Let's have a short walk to cool down, and then get back to our work."

"I don't *want* to work." Noreen pouted.

"Not right now, I know, but soon you will. Come." Claire put her arm around Noreen and led her out of the office.

MARCH 6, 1993

One month later

THE SEVEN WOMEN sat in Noreen's and Denny's living room, their meeting place of late. They started referring to the house as Command Central. They usually gathered there because it was convenient, being central yet close to the university, but mostly because Denny was such an extraordinary cook and always prepared the best snacks and meals around.

It had been over one month since Noreen and Claire had been moved down to the main floor with all their lab equipment and books. They were told that the third floor was now off limits. Neither of them had been able to do much work in the new lab. The whole Science Building seemed to have a different feel to it; before it was a friendly, happy place, with lots of sharing of discoveries. It now had a sinister feel. People did not speak to one another. No one knew who was working with whom. Everyone was very cautious. Even Joanie acted as though they didn't know each other if they happened to pass on the stairs. Noreen respected her decision, knew she was afraid, but still wished she could talk with her.

"How are we going to know what's happening up there on the third floor if we aren't even allowed to go up there?" Claire asked.

"Well," Merle answered, "how about this? Fanny and I can try to go up there. No one knows us, no one has seen us, and we're pretty innocent looking, aren't we?" She laughed.

"No, Merle, that's too dangerous," Noreen alleged.

"Nonsense," said Merle. "We'll just go up there to see what we can see. Besides, everyone knows that older women are invisible. We can go anywhere." She smiled sadly.

"You know, that's actually not a bad idea," Jo-Jo contributed to the discussion. "No one does know them. And they are pretty innocent looking."

"Until you get to know them of course," Patty teased.

The women all chuckled.

"Okay, it's settled. Fanny and I are going to the third floor to see what we can see."

"Oh goodie," said Fanny. "Another adventure."

MARCH 9, 1993

Three days later

FANNY AND MERLE walked up the steps and into the Science Building. Fanny wore her purple hat with the large brim, the one she called her spy hat. They walked to the elevator, pressed the up button, got in, and pressed three. To their surprise, the elevator took them right to the third floor. They stepped out into a large hallway, which seemed deserted. There were big windows looking into different labs. They started walking down the hall and noticed that everyone in the labs was packing. People were carefully wrapping lab equipment and putting it all into cartons and wooden crates. They were packing books and notebooks; it seemed as though everything was being wrapped up and put into boxes.

Merle looked at Fanny. "I don't think these are the people who usually work here. They're dressed differently. Something's off."

"Hey!" a voice boomed out behind them. "Who are you? What are you doing here?"

"Oh, hello, young man." Fanny smiled sweetly at the security guard. "I believe we might be lost. We're looking for the Senior Ladies Association. I believe it used to meet here on the third floor, but now I'm not so sure."

"Well, it doesn't meet here now." The man started ushering them towards the elevator, not quite touching them, but very close.

Merle turned around to look at him. "Do you know where it might be meeting?"

"Have no idea. But you can't be here. This is a restricted area."

"Restricted. Oh my," said Fanny. "Restricted, Merle. Imagine that."

"I was sure the Senior Ladies Association was meeting here." Merle turned away from the guard and looked down the corridor. "Are you sure, young man, that it is not somewhere on this floor?"

The security guard sighed and gently put a hand on each of their shoulders and propelled them towards the elevator.

"I'm sure the notice for the meeting said third floor." Fanny swung around and out from under his hand. She walked in the other direction, looking into the rooms she passed.

"Hey, come back here," the guard hollered. "Listen, ladies, maybe it said third floor, but probably third floor in another building. This is the Science Building and there is *no* meeting up here. Do you see any other senior ladies? No. That's because your meeting is somewhere else. Now please, get in the elevator and go," he said in a raised voice.

Fanny and Merle took one last look around and then headed into the elevator.

A man walked up to the elevator door. "What's happening, George?"

"Oh, nothing, Dr. Clovis," the guard said. "These two little old ladies were looking for a meeting and were lost. Quite harmless."

"THEY'RE PACKING? WHY are they packing?" Noreen asked, after Fanny and Merle returned to the house. "They just moved in there a few months ago."

"They are packing everything; lab equipment, books, the works. There are cartons everywhere. Not only are they packing," Merle continued, "I didn't see anyone who looked like undergrad or post-doc scientists. They all seemed to be security guards or something. They were all older than the usual students and they definitely dressed differently."

"That's so strange." Claire straightened out the pen on the coffee table, making it exactly perpendicular with the edge. "Something new is going on."

"Look, we haven't exactly figured out what the something old was that was going on before. And now this." Noreen sat back sullenly.

"Do you think we should notify the authorities?" asked Merle.

"Which authorities did you have in mind? We already know the government is involved with Clovis and his work with the Sertoli cells and the new virus. If the government supports him, you can bet they're not going to listen to us, no matter what we tell them." Noreen adjusted the brown and gold pillow behind her back.

Jo-Jo took a sip of her beer. "Maybe it's time to pay another visit to that lab before those cartons all go somewhere."

"Oh, I think it would be too dangerous," Noreen declared. "Not like last time. Now they are guarding everything more than ever before."

"I still think we can do it. If we go in on a Saturday night, late, there will only be a few guards. We can cause a diversion in one place, and get into the lab that way. We have to try *something*."

MARCH 13, 1993

Four days later

THE FOLLOWING SATURDAY night all seven women, all dressed in black, except for the purple of Fanny's spy hat, stood huddled in the parking lot.

"Okay," Jo-Jo whispered. "Is everyone sure she knows what to do?" The women nodded.

"Good," said Jo-Jo. "Wait here until I unlock the front door. Once I've signalled you, come quickly and quietly into the building. Then we'll start."

Jo-Jo walked in the shadows to the front door of the Science Building and quickly got the door open. The others followed her path and eased into the building. It was very quiet. Noreen's and Claire's lab was just down the hall, and they headed there.

"Now, we're not sure if the security guards are following their usual route or not," Jo-Jo whispered, once they were in the lab. "Everything here changes so quickly. Noreen, Denny, ready?"
Noreen nodded. She and Denny went out the front door. After Jo-Jo relocked it from the inside and left, Noreen and Denny started banging on the outside door.

"Let us in. Can someone please let us in?" They pushed the buzzer for security over and over. "We need to get in!"

After a short time, lights brightened the front entrance and two security guards came to the door.

"What's going on here?" one of them yelled. "Go away. It's after hours. Who are you, anyway?"

"I'm sorry, you don't know me, but I am Dr. Noreen Stanton, and my lab is on the first floor of this building. Here is my ID." She held out her university ID card. "I have a bit of an emergency. I left some very important medical papers in my office by mistake and I need to get them. My mother is in the hospital and I have to take those papers there right away. It's really urgent. Can you please let me in to retrieve them? This is my friend Denny who drove me. Please, let me in for just a minute. I won't be long at all."

THE OTHER WOMEN ran up the stairs. Three actually ran, Fanny and Merle walked, but they were both quite fit and had no problem reaching the third floor. They were again to act as lookouts while the others checked the labs. They also watched the elevator. They figured the guards were lazy and would take the elevator rather than the stairs.

Jo-Jo let Claire and Patty into one large lab and went to open the doors of a few other rooms. They rushed from room to room, taking in as much as they could.

"The elevator, it's moving," Fanny whispered loudly. Hurry." They all hit the stairwell just as the elevator door opened again.

"That was some strange lady, that Doctor, wasn't she?" one of the guards remarked.

"Yep, she sure was. Glad it wasn't anything to do with this floor or we would've really been in trouble. How about a game of cribbage to pass the time?"

"Sounds good. This is quite a boring job, isn't it? Nothing ever really happens around here." And with that, the two guards sat down to their game.

THE WOMEN WENT BACK to Noreen's and Denise's house, Command Central. Even though it was very late at night, they still had to pick up their cars as they had all gone to the university together.

"Okay, they definitely are moving somewhere. But where?" Claire pondered.

"Was everything packed up?" Noreen asked.

"You wouldn't believe it. Everything. All the equipment, all the books, notes, everything. But there was no address on any of the boxes. Not one. No sign at all that we could see where all this stuff was going." Claire methodically buttoned and unbuttoned her jacket.

"Well," Denny piped in, "I suggest everyone go home and we all get some sleep. We can think on this and watch what happens this week."

"Good idea." Merle stood up and Fanny joined her. "We're getting too old to stay up this late."

"Good thing I had my nap today," said Fanny. "We'll see you all next week. It's been another exciting adventure."

"Yes, it has," said Merle. "We lookouts now bid adieu to the look-ins."

They smiled as they walked to the door.

"Denny, what do you think is going on here?" Noreen asked after the others had all left.

"I really have no idea. You would know better than I. But I don't think it looks good. First, you find out Clovis is working with Sertoli cells and has a virus to make only males. Then Joanie tells you there is another virus that can make only females. Then you find out the government and the army are involved. That lab is restricted, so they must be doing something that the army wants but doesn't want us to know about. And now they are moving somewhere."

"Yep, that about sums it up." Noreen sighed as she plopped down on the sofa. "I don't have a good feeling about this. And besides, all this stuff with Clovis is on my brain, and Claire's too. We can't even concentrate enough to do our own work in that new little lab they stuck us in."

"The thing that puzzles me the most is that this is supposed to be a democracy. Things like this just don't happen in this country without the public knowing about it. It seems like a bad dream of some sort."

"Mmm." Noreen nodded.

"Well, let's go to bed, sweetie. Things have a way of sorting themselves out. Sooner or later, everything will become obvious."

"Yeah, I guess you're right." Noreen pushed up from the sofa and walked down the hall with Denise. "But y'know, I'm really worried. This is serious. Something big is going on here, and I don't feel we can ignore it. Do you?"

"No, I don't. But tomorrow is another day. Things may look clearer in the morning. Let's pack it in for tonight."

"I'm tired. So very tired." Noreen stretched. "But I'm really, really concerned."

MARCH 15, 1993

Two days later

ON MONDAY MORNING, Claire arrived early as she usually did to find the steps leading up to the Science Building cordoned off with yellow strips and police milling around.

"What's going on, officer?" she asked a young policewoman standing by the police tape. "I work here. I need to get to my lab inside."

"I'm sorry, ma'am," the officer replied. "There was a fire here yesterday. Apparently the whole third floor was destroyed. The fire department is checking the building now to determine whether it is safe for anyone to go in."

"A fire? Here? Oh my goodness. Was anyone hurt?"

"I'm sorry, but we're not at liberty to discuss that with anyone, Miss—what is your name?"

"Doctor. Dr. Claire Christopher. I used to work on the third floor, but now my lab is on the first floor. Was there any damage to the first floor?"

"I'm not sure, Dr. Christopher. If you wait, there will be an announcement at nine-thirty and a press conference as well."

"That's in an hour and a half," Claire mused. "I think I'll go over to the library and come back here for nine-thirty. Thank you, officer."

"You're welcome, Doctor. See you later."

Claire went into the library and stopped at the row of telephones to tell Noreen about the fire. She asked her to let the others know. Noreen said she would be right over.

AT NINE-THIRTY, CLAIRE and Noreen stood on the bottom step of the Science Building, just behind the police tape. A crowd had gathered, students, scientists, reporters, and the curious. They could see Jo-Jo, Denise, and Patty in the crowd. Fanny and Merle joined them.

A very tall and extensively decorated soldier approached the microphone that was set up at the top of the stairs. He looked over the growing crowd and cleared his throat. "Ladies and gentlemen, my name is General Sonderman. The police and fire department have been involved with this incident since yesterday. The army was called in to assist as well, which is why I am here today. The president of the university has asked me to give this briefing. I will give you a quick review of what occurred here over the last twenty-four hours. Yesterday, at approximately four p.m., a fire broke out on the third floor. The fire department was able to contain it, but not before all the labs and their contents were completely destroyed. I am very sorry to have to report that there was one fatality."

There was a murmur in the crowd.

"Because it was Sunday, no one should have been in the building. But apparently one of the scientists was in his lab. It is with great regret that I inform you that Dr. Cleve Clovis has perished in the fire."

The crowd let out a collective moan. Everyone seemed to talk at once. General Sonderman let the crowd express itself for a few minutes.

"Please, ladies and gentlemen, just give me a few more minutes here. I know how difficult all this must be for you. I've heard that Dr. Clovis was a wonderful scientist."

"That he wasn't," Noreen muttered to Claire, "but he still shouldn't have died."

General Sonderman cleared his throat again. "Please, let's have a bit of quiet here for just a minute or two more. Just as soon as the fire department has finished their complete inspection, we will let you know when access to the building will be available. That should be sometime later today. For now, we ask all those who work here to be patient. We will let you back in just as soon as it is safe to do so. There will, of course, be a memorial for Dr. Clovis and you will be hearing more about that fairly soon. We ask you to disperse quickly and quietly and stand away from the steps and the police tape so that the police, fire department, and army can all do their jobs. We will make another announcement here to bring you up to date at three-thirty this afternoon. Thank you and good morning." General Sonderman turned off the microphone and quickly walked away.

Claire and Noreen backed off the step and went to join the other women.

"I'm stunned." Noreen took Denny's hand. "I hated the jerk, I really did, but I sure didn't wish him dead. And in a fire too. What a terrible way to go."

"C'mon, let's go." Jo-Jo herded the women away from the crowd. "I think we could all use a coffee and some down time."

"Wait a minute." Noreen stopped short. "There's Joanie. Hey, Joanie, would you like to join us for coffee?"

Joanie looked frightened. She turned to where General Sonderman was talking to some other soldiers, looked at him for a few seconds, shook her head no, and quickly turned and walked away.

"What the hell are they doing to those folks?" Noreen asked. "She is clearly terrified to be seen with us. Why?"

"Coffee, Noreen, let's get our coffee. Joanie will connect with us when she can." Denny took Noreen's hand and led her down the path. "What's really strange," she looked around at the others, "is the presence of the army. Why aren't people asking why the army is here? It should just be the fire department, police, and the university administration. What on earth has the army got to do with any of this?"

MARCH 26, 1993

Eleven days later

THE MEMORIAL FOR Dr. Clovis was held at the university eleven days after the fire. It was heavily attended. The president of the university, Dr. Phillip Weber, gave the eulogy. A few of Clovis' ex-students spoke. Mostly people came out of curiosity. It seemed everybody on campus was talking about the fire and the fatality. The fact that Clovis, who left his work at five p.m. sharp every day, was there on a Sunday was unusual. The fact that he was the only scientist in the building was also strange. The General had told the crowd at the afternoon press conference that there had been two security guards in the building at the time of the fire, but they were both in the basement. When they smelled the smoke, they called the fire department, but by the time they got there, it was too late for Dr. Clovis, who somehow had gotten trapped in his lab and couldn't get out in time. It was all very peculiar.

Denise, who had come to the memorial to support Noreen who felt obligated to go, summed it up as they were leaving. "It just doesn't add up; things just don't make sense."

APRIL 12, 1993

Seventeen days later

THREE WEEKS AFTER the fire Noreen and Claire were working away in their first floor lab. The second and third floors of the building were off limits, as they were being renovated after the fire. The scientists who worked with Dr. Clovis had been temporarily moved to another building on campus to work with another geneticist, a Dr. Swiftsure, who neither Noreen nor Claire knew. This in itself seemed curious since Noreen and Claire had been involved in the genetic scientific community for decades now, and thought that they knew pretty much all senior academic geneticists in the country; in the world, in fact.

Every time Noreen saw Joanie on campus, she smiled a greeting and was prepared to stop, but Joanie always kept walking, acting as though she didn't know her. Her face was drawn and haggard; in fact, she looked terrible, Noreen thought. She used to be a fun person, and Noreen had enjoyed her company. She wished she could help her somehow. She couldn't understand why Joanie was acting like this now that Clovis was no longer in the picture.

Over the next few weeks, things settled into a routine. Noreen and Claire began working in earnest. Sometimes days went by when they didn't talk about Clovis or the fire. They had their own projects they were working on and were excited about their new line of research.

JUNE 29, 1993

Two and a half months later

TRYING TO FIGURE out what was going on with Clovis and the army took time, which enabled Patty and Jo-Jo to become good friends. In fact, all seven women had grown closer. Jo-Jo's life had changed radically since her move to Calgary from New York.

Once Jo-Jo got involved with helping to break into Clovis' lab, she spent less time with the STALAG bunch and more time with her new acquaintances.

These women were trailblazers, innovative and original and besides, they enjoyed dinner parties, delicious food and wine, intriguing books, intelligent conversation, and she was honoured that they had made her a part of their group. They were so incredibly different than the women of STALAG, she thought with a warm feeling in her heart for her new friends. Just the kind of women she had been looking for.

"I REALLY LIKE this one." Jo-Jo nodded as she looked at some of the new work in Patty's studio. She stopped, scratched her short, dark blonde hair, cocked her head, and stepped back to further contemplate a painting: a large group of women standing on the round globe of the world, all quite realistically painted. The women were all colours, all shapes, but every one of them, on the left side, had a little external heart from which trickled a small stream of red.

"Not too many people will like this one, I think," said Patty. "It's not very subtle, like some of the others. But I really felt I wanted to do this one."

"I can understand why. I like it a lot." Jo-Jo smiled.

Patty enjoyed Jo-Jo's insights, and Jo-Jo loved discussing art with another intelligent woman as they continued to discuss Patty's new work in the studio.

"WE'LL JUST HAVE to sit tight and see what develops." Merle took a sip of her tea. She and Fanny never tired of discussing their "spy days" as Fanny called them.

"Yes, surely something will occur before long. I just have a funny feeling about this whole Clovis thing." Fanny stirred another sugar lump into her tea.

"Yeah, me too. Something is bound to happen soon. I'm quite concerned, you know."

"You're right. I'm worried too." Fanny took another sip of tea. "In fact, I do think something will happen soon, as you say. Very soon. Far too many things are still unexplained and this story is far from over."

"Chirpy chirp," said Bunjie.

"See? Even Bunjie agrees with us." Fanny smiled at the little bird.

NOREEN LOOKED OUT the window of her new lab.

"Well, that may be the only advantage to being down here," she murmured under her breath. "At least we can clearly see what's going on out there."

Just as she muttered that sentiment, she saw Swiftsure and that General walking together, laughing. The General put his arm around Swiftsure's shoulder and they laughed again. They waved goodbye to each other as Swiftsure walked up the stairs to the Science Building and the General walked off towards the parking lot.

"What are those two laughing about?" she asked a group of test tubes on the counter. "What the hell is so funny?" She was angry.

Claire walked into the lab. "Hi. What's up?"

"That damn army. Stupid Swiftsure. That's up. I just saw the General and that Swiftsure being all buddy-buddy. First it's that General and Clovis; now him and that Swiftsure. Why are they even friends? What's going on here?"

"Nori, leave it. We don't care. Let's just concentrate on our own work and forget about Clovis, Swiftsure, and the General."

"I don't want to forget about it. How can I? It's in my face every second, especially since we've been down here in this stupid first-floor lab. And besides, what's the army doing at the university anyway? Claire, this is Canada. Canada. For Pete's sake. We don't do armies. We don't do violence. And in this building, we do science. Science. Not wars."

Claire walked over to Noreen and put her arm around her. "Look, I'm upset too. But what can we do? The best thing we can do is our own work, right? Let's concentrate on that and try to forget about Clovis for even a little while. Okay?"

Noreen turned her head, but Claire walked around to face her.

"Okay?" she asked again, looking into her eyes.

"Yeah, yeah, okay," Noreen quietly grumbled, and turned to her workspace.

JULY 9, 1993

Ten days later

IT WAS JO-JO'S first Stampede ever. She decided to really *do* it her first year and take in as much of the festivities as she could. On the first day she went to the Stampede Parade. She was delighted that Denise invited her to join them, as they all had tickets in the Bleachers on 9th Avenue where the three hour spectacle would pass by.

It was a great day for the Parade, cloudless sky, warm but not too hot sun, mountains could be seen far off in the distance, with just a tip of snow on their peaks. Patty had brought some oranges for them all, to go with the basket of food Denise had packed.

"Be careful with these," Patty told Jo-Jo. "They're full of vodka."

Jo-Jo raised her eyebrows in a question.

"Oh, it's a trick I learned from my doctor friend, Ruth. She just fills syringes with vodka, and then injects the oranges. That way, we can bring the oranges with us, without drinking in public."

Jo-Jo laughed as she took one, and settled down to watch the Parade. She later told her mother, who had been too ill to go, that she learned how to wave her cowboy hat and yell, "Yahoo!" She even demonstrated it, laughing with Marcy.

That first morning was one wonderful thing after another. Jo-Jo had never seen so many horses, especially in the city. She was stunned to see the Percherons, and the Clydesdales, especially after Denise told her one horse usually weighed more than two thousand pounds or one ton. And the Indians—hundreds of Indians, all in full regalia, some in long feathered headdresses which reached all the way to the ground. And Jo-Jo just loved how their horses were loose and followed along, including the young colts who just stayed with their mothers; no leads, ropes, nothing. Jo-Jo couldn't believe that they wouldn't run away.

"Oh, they never run away, they always stay with their herd,"

Denise told her. "We've been coming now for, gosh, I don't know. How long, Nori?"

"Decades," said Noreen, biting into an orange and squirting juice all over her freckled face.

Everyone around her burst out laughing as the juice/vodka trickled over her freckles.

"But we've only been sitting in the bleachers like this for maybe eight years. They didn't always have them."

"And it's a good thing they do have them," Fanny piped up. "Or else Merle and I likely wouldn't be here with you."

Jo-Jo couldn't believe that even Fanny and Merle wore cowboy hats. It seemed as though the entire city went crazy. Fanny's cowboy hat had purple and pink feathers around the hatband. She wore a red and white checkered shirt, a long denim skirt, and blue boots. She looked very different, as did Merle, in her Levi's and blue and white Western shirt and white hat.

"What the hell is that?" Noreen yelled, pointing down 9th Avenue as the parade was going by.

"What? What are you looking at, hon?" Denise craned her neck in the direction Noreen was pointing.

"It's the bloody army. It's the goddamn army in the Stampede parade. What is going on here? That army is everywhere. In the Science Building, at the university, and now in the parade."

"Nori, they are usually in the parade. Every year. You probably just didn't notice them so much before. It's not such a big deal. Look."

Just after a group of men wearing kilts and playing the bagpipes, identifying themselves as The Grampian Police Pipe Band from Aberdeen, Scotland, they saw the military. The infantry led the way for a large truck and a dozen jeeps full of men in camo army clothes, all wearing white cowboy hats. On the lead truck was a large sign which stated: "The Canadian Army, Sarcee Trail Base, celebrates Stampede with all Calgarians."

"Well, I don't celebrate Stampede with you," Noreen grumbled.

"Hush." Denise put her hand on Noreen's thigh. "Not here. It's inappropriate. Just enjoy the parade."

"But, they're everywhere. Can't we even go to Stampede without the army being in our faces?"

"Look, your problem is with one particular person in the army, right? And he's not even here. Watch the trick riders over there. You like them."

Slowly Noreen forgot about the army and went back into Stampede mode.

"Yee-haw!"

"Look, here comes Scotty again. You always like Scotty."

"Who is Scotty?" asked Jo-Jo.

"Scotty is about eighty years old, and he trains his sheepdogs," Denise explained. "Watch this" and she indicated the scene that was coming towards them. Jo-Jo watched in amazement as an entire herd of sheep came down the street, controlled only by three sheepdogs.

The dogs would have the sheep turn in a circle, or go to one side or the other. Old Scotty just slowly ambled along with his long pole in his hand, emitting the odd whistle to his incredibly well-trained dogs.

"Wow." Jo-Jo was really enjoying herself a lot, perhaps slightly helped by the second orange she had eaten and imbibed. "Look, the oldest pioneer lady ever." She pointed to a black buggy with a fringe on the top. "Bert Miguelon," she read off the sign on the buggy. She wondered what it must have been like to be a pioneer on the prairies so very many decades ago. She didn't wonder for too long as another sign caught her eye.

"Oh my," exclaimed Jo-Jo. "Is that really true?"

"Is what true?" asked Patty.

"Look, it says Kit Carson Cody—Buffalo Bill's grandson."

"Well, if that's what it says, then that's who it is. Pretty cool, eh?"

To answer her properly, Jo-Jo waved her white hat. She had decided to go with the good guys.

AS STAMPEDE WEEK went on, it became clear to Jo-Jo that the Parade was only the beginning of the cowboy craziness. The women took Jo-Jo to the Palliser Hotel one evening. They walked through the very elegant lobby of the hotel where the Queen had once stayed, now strewn with hay bales, wooden fences, and other western paraphernalia. A noisy, lively and friendly mood prevailed. They walked into the ballroom which had been converted into a giant saloon renamed the Paralizer for the occasion and sat down at a table near the stage. The place was stuffed out, as Jo-Jo later recalled for Marcy. The round tables were all very close to one another, most of which had several jugs of beer on them.

Patty got a large pitcher of beer and Claire helped by balancing seven glasses to bring to their table. Almost immediately, four men, all dressed in Western wear as was most everyone else there, joined them. Noreen explained to Jo-Jo that there were no such things as strangers during Stampede. Everyone sat together.

"Hi." one of the men said. "Happy Stampede to you ladies."

"And Happy Stampede to you gentlemen." Patty raised her glass and took a swig of beer.

Noreen and Claire were very intently whispering to each other. After a few minutes, Noreen turned to one of the men.

"I don't mean to seem rude, and trust me, this is not a come-on, but don't we know you? You look so familiar."

"Well," the man answered, "my name is Dave. David Weber."

"Weber? Any relation to Phillip Weber?"

The man turned to his friends and smiled. "Calgary truly is a small town, isn't it?" He looked at Noreen and Claire. "Yes, Phillip Weber is my brother. I take it you know him. Do you know him well?"

"Fairly well," Noreen answered. "We," she indicated herself and Claire, "have worked at the university for a long time now. We see him now and again. Nice man."

"Well, I think so, but then, I guess I'm a bit partial to my family."

"What do you do, David? Do you work at the University?"

David did not have time to answer because of a commotion at the front entrance.

"Look!" someone yelled and pointed to the door.

Jo-Jo could not believe her eyes. There, in the doorway, was a cowboy sitting astride a large palomino horse, easing his way into the room, which was proving to be quite difficult since the tables were all so close together. Everyone in the room was laughing and cheering. Several security people came up to him and he leaned over across the saddle to talk to them. The men all laughed, and then the cowboy, waving a white hat, slowly turned his horse around and walked him out back through the lobby of the hotel, to the loud cheers and applause of the many hundreds of people in the room.

"I wouldn't have believed that if I hadn't seen it with my own eyes." Jo-Jo shook her head in disbelief. "This city is insane."

"There'll be entertainment soon," Patty explained to Jo-Jo. "I'll never forget, years ago, I saw k.d. lang and the Reclines perform here, before they were famous. No one had ever even heard of them. I heard the first set and stayed to watch them again. And again. They were so good. That was in the days when k.d. lang said she was the incarnation of Patsy Cline. And she always wore these nylons with a run in them. Years later, when she was performing at the Calgary Centre for Performing Arts, she had to go on stage, and the stage manager told me that she was late getting onto the stage because she had trouble getting the right rips in her nylons."

They all laughed. "Oh, here they come." Patty nodded toward the stage. She took off her white cowboy hat, waved it in the air, and yelled, "Yee-haw!"

Jo-Jo laughed but then looked around and most of the people in the room were doing just what Patty did. "Yee-haw!" came from everywhere. Even Fanny and Merle Yee-Haw-ed.

Oh well. Jo-Jo doffed her hat. "Yee-haw!"

Patty burst out laughing. "Now you got it, Jo-Jo. Happy Stampede to you!"

After that, between the noises of the crowd, twanging of the guitars, plucking of the banjos, banging of the drums, any talking or even shouting to each other was impossible, but drinking beer and yelling and trying to dance when there was no room other than on the tops of the tables was *de rigueur* for the rest of the evening. Even Fanny and Merle seemed to enjoy it although they drank very little beer, and did not leave their seats.

THE REST OF the Stampede was just as much fun as the first few days. Every place in the city was decorated in a western theme.

They went to pancake breakfasts. Twice, they square danced in the mall. Jo-Jo found it easy to learn and she really liked the dancing. All the women went down to the Stampede grounds many times. They saw the rodeo and the chuck wagon races. They went to the evening show at the grandstand. They walked down the mid-way and even went on some of the rides. Jo-Jo's favourite part was the stables full of all kinds of animals, cows, pigs, sheep, chickens, turkeys, and of course, horses. She loved the fair where foods and preserves were on display, and all the art work—there was so much to see and her friends were anxious to show her as much as possible. She later told Marcy she was happy that Stampede was only ten days because she didn't think she had the energy for much more. Besides after ten days, she was a mite tired of waving her cowboy hat and yelling yahoo or yee-haw. She was happy to put it away until the following year.

JULY 12, 1993

That same week

THE ARMY JET taxied down the runway. General Sonderman, unlit cigar stuffed in his mouth, sat frowning out the window as the jet began its ascent. He saw the tropical beach with long stretches of sand bordered by ocean and palm trees. He noticed the group of buildings not far from the water and the soldiers around them and the entire island. It was just large enough to have six bunk houses, two private cabins, a bath and shower area, a workshop cum lab, and a large mess and recreation room. There was still room left over for a person to walk along the beach or in the woods. He could distinguish a man sitting in a chair on the beach, drink in hand. He could almost see Clovis' smile from up high. This has worked out well, he thought. Clovis is happy being here, and his work is almost finished. The army will have genetic weaponry now, thanks to this project. He just wasn't sure what to do with Clovis after this was all over.

Maybe he could start him working on some new projects. Clovis had been on the island now for four months, and although he said he enjoyed being there, he had started mentioning "going back", whatever that meant to him. Sonderman did not want him to return to Calgary, at least, not for a long time, long after the General revealed his genetic warfare plans. And he wasn't ready to share them with anyone else just yet.

Clovis was a loner; he lived alone, had no family. It was easier to control the other scientists who used to work with him—he had just threatened their families. Every one of them capitulated and did exactly as Sonderman asked, for fear that harm would come to their parents, wives, children. Sonderman thought that was just the price of war. Even in Canada, they were always at war with someone. These days it was those damn females, who think they belong everywhere. He was a General in the army, and he had to be in control. He was pleased that he didn't have to follow through on his threats, as yet, that everyone had done what he had asked, or rather, demanded. But Clovis—what kind of leverage could he use with him?

The plane picked up altitude and speed and headed back on the long trip to Calgary.

CLOVIS PUT HIS drink down and looked out over the water.

"This is the life," he said. Although he usually uttered that particular sentiment daily, he meant it less and less as time went on. He spent most of the day on the beach. About three p.m., he generally went into his cabin, showered, and went to the lab. He had a staff of four on the island and he went over their work with them. He stayed at the lab for three or four hours, and then went to the main dining room for dinner. Once a week, he spoke with Swiftsure, the guy who was running his Calgary lab. They were doing ancillary work for Clovis that was going well too. Clovis had trained those scientists and knew them all. Swiftsure he wasn't so sure about; he had never heard of him before. The General had brought him into the project.

Clovis was relaxed, tanned, feeling good, but one thing troubled him greatly. General Sonderman had told him he would be famous. He wondered when that might happen. Right now, most people thought he had died in the fire. He smiled at that thought. They had really fooled the whole university. The whole city, in fact. By the time they had that memorial service for him, he was long gone.

Ushered out of the building just before the fire, Clovis never saw what became of the third floor. All the equipment he would need, his notes, anything relevant to his work, had already been shipped to the island earlier that Sunday. Several men from General Sonderman's special forces escorted him directly to the waiting plane. The General explained that he had to remain at the university to make sure that everything went according to their plans. Everything had worked out very well. But when would this *famous* thing click in? he wondered. He tried to discuss it with the General this morning before he left, but the General just changed the subject. Clovis wondered what would happen once the project was completely over. They were very close now to finishing up with what the General wanted. He took another sip of his drink and stretched out in the warm sun.

JULY 13, 1993

Next day

WALKING DOWN THE path on the campus from the library to the Science Building, Noreen saw Joanie coming toward her. She smiled sadly, thinking Joanie would walk right by, ignoring her as she usually did. But as Joanie approached, her eyes flicked up to Noreen.

"Coffee?" she whispered.

"Now?"

"Yeah, but we have to go where no one can see us."

Once they were settled in The Red and White, a small café far from campus, Joanie put both hands around her tall glass of iced tea, with her eyes lowered. "He threatened to harm my mother. He said they were going to do terrible things to her."

"Wait. Who threatened? Who said that?"

"That General. The one who announced Clovis' death. He spoke to everyone in our lab."

"Oh my God. How's your mother?"

"My mother died last month."

"Oh, Joanie, I'm so sorry to hear that." Noreen put her hand over Joanie's, which was resting on the white and red checkered tablecloth.

"She was sick anyway. Her death was not unexpected. But I didn't want her to have any more pain and I felt sure that General would hurt her if I said anything. Now they can't hurt her."

"But, they can still hurt you," Noreen said.

"Yes, they can. But I can't stand this anymore. And if I can get out of this, even if they did hurt me, it'd be worth it."

"What's going on? Clovis is dead. Didn't all this stop when he died?"

"No, that's the problem. It didn't. They just moved us to another lab after the fire. But we're supposed to go back to the third floor sometime next month. An army scientist who calls himself a geneticist is in charge, but really, it's all the same kind of work we were doing before. It's as though he's become Clovis. Why they want to do that work . . . Well, I know why actually. The army wants to use these viruses as weapons. And I don't want to be a part of it. Not at all. And neither do the other people working at the lab. But all their families have been threatened and we're all so scared. That General Sonderman might seem nice in public but he can be very scary when you're alone with him.

"Something else, too. I don't know, it seems weird. But Sonderman was at our lab last week, and he was talking to the head guy, Swiftsure. They went into the office but the door must not have fully closed. I was leaning over to pick up some papers that fell on the floor and could overhear them talking. I heard them mention Clovis' name. Why would they do that? He's been dead for months now. I mean, it's his work, sure, but they talked about him like he was just around the corner."

"Hmm, that's strange. How d'you think you can get out of that lab?"

"I don't know. I'm thinking of different things. I thought about sick leave, but they said if anyone got sick and had to leave, the army doctors would be treating them. That actually scares me. I think I might just go up to the boss and tell him I don't want to work there anymore and see what happens. I'm still trying to think it out."

"Well, if there's anything at all I can do for you, you'll let me know, right?"

"Yeah, I will," Joanie said. "Just knowing you're around is helpful. I think we should meet again if we can. I'm prepared to take the chance. They're not overly watchful these days anyway. Not like before."

"Okay, if you think it's safe enough for you. That would be great."

They agreed to meet again in ten days. Joanie said by then she would have a plan ready for leaving.

JULY 23, 1993

Ten days later

"SHE WAS ALMOST murdered. I just know they tried to murder her!" Joanie burst out as soon as Noreen slid into the red vinyl booth of The Red and White where they had agreed to have their meetings.

"Whoa. Who was almost murdered?" Noreen slipped off her denim jacket.

"Angie. Angie was almost murdered."

"Oh, c'mon. Angie was hit by a car in the parking lot. Everyone here knows that. It was an accident." Noreen fiddled with the small jukebox against the wall over their table. She loved this little cafe, meant to emulate a 1960s joint. There were red and white checkered cloths on the tables, and the food was served in little baskets. But for their purposes today, it was small, quiet, and away from the University where they were unlikely to meet anyone they knew.

"That's what they want you to think. I know they tried to murder her. And they almost succeeded. She's been in ICU since they did it."

"Look, you're getting a bit paranoid here. We know she was hit by a car."

"Yes, she was." Joanie wiped the tears from her eyes. "Listen, last Sunday—"

"Wait," Noreen interrupted, "you mean Sunday, the day she was run over by that car?"

"Yeah. That Sunday. So that day, about four in the afternoon, Angie phones me."

"She phoned you at home?" Noreen asked.

"Yes." Joanie sighed impatiently. "She phoned me at home. She said she just had a call from Swiftsure . . ."

"Who?" Noreen leaned forward.

"Swiftsure, you know, my boss, the guy that took over Clovis' job."

"Oh, yeah, Swiftsure . . ."

"Yeah. Well, anyway, she said she got a call from him, and he asked her to come to the lab early that evening to drop something off. She said it was kinda silly, that it could've easily waited until Monday morning. She wondered what she should do. We talked about it, and then she decided it would only take a few minutes to drop off that paper, so she would go. I agreed with her. So she went, and that's when she was run over."

"You mean that's when the accident happened," Noreen interrupted.

"No, that's when she was almost killed. And now she's in ICU. No one knows if she'll recover. And I could have told her to stay home. I feel responsible, you know. I'm sure that accident was deliberate. You know why?" Joanie answered her own question. "Because she told me a week before that she was going to tell everyone what was going on in that lab. She told Swiftsure that she wanted out and you know they won't let anyone leave. So when he told her she couldn't leave, she told him she was going to start talking. *That's* why she was run over."

Noreen leaned forward, deep in thought. Joanie could be right. What if Angie was run over on purpose?

"And," Joanie took a deep breath, "you know that I was going to do that myself. We talked about it just ten days ago at this very table. I was going to get out, to start talking. In fact, I mentioned something to Swiftsure already. Angie just beat me to it."

"Well, that's not the only thing she did first," Noreen mentioned sardonically.

Joanie looked up disapprovingly.

Noreen pushed her red hair off her forehead. "So you think they really want to keep things secret, eh?"

"I *know* they do. I'm sure of it. And I think that Angie was becoming a threat to Swiftsure and all the others. We can't talk to the administration at all because they're in on whatever it is they're doing. I don't really know what's going on, but I know something is not right." Joanie sat back with tears in her eyes.

Noreen put her hand on Joanie's arm.

"Joanie, thanks. Thanks for telling me this, thanks for being brave enough to meet with me. You know, we'll do whatever we can for you and the rest of the folks trapped in that lab."

Joanie knew she meant Denise and the others. They had talked about how they all wanted to help many times in the past few months.

"Thanks." Joanie's voice softened, and she let the tears come. "This is getting way too involved for me. I don't want to be here. I don't know what to do."

"Do nothing for right now. We'll figure this out, pretty soon. We've been coasting along lately, but we'll start looking into things a lot more now. I really thought Angie had an accident. But I see what you're saying though. It's probably true, that they wanted to silence her. When she wouldn't be quiet, they silenced her their own way." Noreen shook her head in disbelief. "Jeez!"

JULY 29, 1993

One week later

CLOVIS LEANED BACK on his desk chair. It had been more than two weeks since he last talked with General Sonderman. His work here on this island was pretty much complete. Now what would happen? How would he become famous? The General had promised him that this work would make him famous but how was that even possible if everything was supposed to be such a damn secret? Who would ever know he was involved? They all thought he was dead. How was he going to get out of this? Secretly he wished he had more of an imagination. He would never admit this to a living soul, or even a dead one, he chuckled at his perceived humour, but he didn't have a great imagination. He couldn't figure out how he would get off this island, come back to life, and become famous. He sure hoped the General had a plan. And he hoped he had this plan soon.

"I'm not staying here for much longer," Clovis murmured.. "Nice as it is." He smiled out the window at the beach, smelling the salty ocean air which always made him feel good. "Enough of this island stuff. I wanna go home to Calgary. And I *really* wanna be famous. Famous is what I want. Famous and rich."

The first time the General gave him money, his eyes almost betrayed his incredible surprise. It took all he could muster within himself being cool about receiving any amount. Each time he got better at it. He was a scientist after all, and he wasn't used to being paid anything other than a not very lucrative salary. Now that he had money in his pocket, the pocket in his elegant new clothes, he chuckled again, he wanted to focus on being famous.

"I'll show those girls. Heh, heh." He chortled. "They will be so surprised. Finally, it will be me, me, who does something clever. Not them. Me!"

There was a knock on the door. "Dr. Clovis."

"Come in."

"Dr. Clovis, one of the soldiers wants to talk with you."

"Okay, bring him in." Clovis sat up straight and waited.

"Dr. Clovis," the soldier, wearing pressed army khaki shorts and a clean short-sleeve uniform top, began, "we have just heard from the General. He'll be back in about ten days and he hopes that everything will be wrapped up by then. Is that possible?"

Clovis thought for a moment. They were really pretty much finished now, he knew, so sure, he could pretend to be done when they wanted him to be done.

"Yes, I could arrange to have everyone work hard to complete the work within ten days. And then what?"

"Why, and then we leave." The soldier smiled. "Don't you want to get back to civilization, nice as all this is?"

"Yes," Clovis answered. "I'll be happy to get back, indeed."

After the soldier had given him more details and departed, Clovis wondered what getting back would mean for him. Whenever he tried to talk about it with the General, he was told not to worry about it, that the army would arrange everything for him. Arrange what kinds of things, he wondered.

JULY 30, 1993

One day later

"YOU WANTED TO see me, sir?" The special agent poked his head around the door to General Sonderman's office.

"Yes, I did, Lester, c'mon in."

The soldier entered the office, carefully shut the door, and took a seat across from the desk. He was a muscular, tall man, though not quite as tall as the General. He had a considerable scar running from his left eye to his chin. He was in clean, neatly pressed army fatigues. He waited patiently, hands folded, for the General to address him. When the General finished talking, Lester sat straight up in his chair and put his thick hands on the desk.

"Another one, sir?"

"Yeah, I just heard from Swiftsure, and we're going to need to arrange another accident.

"It seems that there is one more person at the university who is threatening to talk. I think if an accident befalls her, that should be a sufficient message to the rest of them, and then we'll all be in the clear after that. They wouldn't dare risk talking after two of them have met with . . . accidents."

"Okay, sir. And who is this person?"

"Her name is . . . where the hell did I put that paper?" General Sonderman shuffled through a pile of papers on his desk. "Oh, here it is. Her name is Joan, I think she goes by Joanie, Grover. Joan Grover. See, it's women who are the troublemakers. Only the women; never the men. Let's do something a little different than a car accident, though. Don't want to repeat the same thing again. We were lucky with the first one. It was during Stampede, so hardly anyone was around that university. Maybe for this one we can arrange to have something fall on her in the lab, something like that, maybe at night when no one is there. They'll get the idea after her accident and then we should be set. Look into it, but don't do anything right now. Be ready to go with a plan when I give the word. Understood?"

"Understood, sir."

"Great, Lester. So what did you think of that ball game last night?"

JULY 31, 1993

One day later

SATURDAY EVENING FOUND all seven women back at Command Central. Denise was called the Executive Chef as everyone appreciated her skill in the kitchen.

The mood in the room, which usually had some levity in spite of the situation, was somber. Noreen was angry. Claire was depressed and fiddled with her pen and note pad, lining them up evenly and then messing them up and starting over again. Even Merle and Fanny were much quieter than usual.

"We've got to do something. *Now*!" Noreen's voice shattered the quiet.

"I agree," said Claire. "This situation is out of hand. Plus, we cannot get any of our work done."

They talked for two hours and made specific action plans for each of them.

AUGUST 2, 1993

Two days later

"OH, BUNJIE." FANNY stood in front of her parakeet while he swung to and fro in his large cage. "Being a spy was fun, Bunjie. All these months, we had so much fun being spies. But now it's not fun anymore. Someone is seriously injured. That girl, Angie, from the Science Building, is in Intensive Care now. The fun is over. We have to get serious. You know what we are going to do now, Bunjie? We're going to use our knowledge to outwit them."

Fanny put on her beret with the gold feather in it and hung her jacket over her arm.

"I'm sorry, my little Bunjie, but I have to leave you. I have much work to do at the library. See you later." And with that, she was out the door.

AUGUST 4, 1993

Two days later

"THE PRESIDENT WILL see you now."

Noreen and Claire were ushered into the large room overlooking the foothills in the distance as Dr. Phillip Weber, the president of the University of Calgary, rose from his chair and warmly greeted them.

"Two of my favourite scientists." He smiled as he indicated with his arm that they all move to a seating area by the window.

"How can I help you two ladies today?" he asked.

Noreen grimaced, took a deep breath and started.

After listening for five minutes without interrupting, President Weber put up his hands, palms outward. "Whoa. Wait a minute here. Are you trying to tell me that this General, from our army, *our* Canadian army, is doing something perhaps illegal, in cahoots with this university?"

Noreen and Claire looked at each other.

"Look, we know this sounds unreal, but all of what we've been telling you has really happened," Claire said. "This is really going on."

"It's more than unreal. It's ridiculous. Look, Claire, you're an intelligent person, right? So how can a man as decorated and upstanding as General Sonderman possibly be involved in anything like you describe?"

"I don't know, but he is," insisted Noreen.

"I think you two have let your imaginations run away with you. Better get those wonderful imaginations working on more genetic discoveries, eh? Look, I hear what you're saying, but really, we know the General is a fine, upstanding representative of the army. You go back to your labs, and keep doing your impressive work there. Leave these things to me." He smiled at them and stood up.

"But . . ." Noreen started and felt Claire's hand squeeze her upper arm. She looked at Claire who very discretely shook her head.

"Thank you, Phillip," Claire said. "Thank you for your time. We appreciate your seeing us today."

"You're very welcome, little lady. You know I always have time for the two of you. Just try not to get too distracted from your work. We continue to have high hopes for you two."

OUTSIDE THE BUILDING, Noreen stamped her foot hard.

"Ow!" she yelled in surprise. "That hurt."

"Don't be silly." Claire smiled. "If you're going to smash your foot onto the ground like that, of course it'll hurt."

"Now what do we do?"

"Let's wait to see what the other women have found out first," Claire wisely counselled.

AUGUST 5, 1993

Next day

FANNY HADN'T BEEN involved with the university library for some years. True, she had spent so much time in the library when she worked there, but realised she had missed concentrating on a particular project. She loved delving deeply into a problem and almost always came up with the answer and more. This General though—getting information on him was proving difficult.

"I didn't work in the library for forty-five years for nothing," she told Bunjie when she got back from the university. "I've been in the library for the past four days. Four full days working there, Bunjie. That's a long time to be away from you, little bird."

Fanny put her briefcase full of papers on the small table and took off her hat.

"And, Bunjie, you know, I found out about that General, I did. But it sure wasn't easy.

"Now, I'm sorry, little Bunjie, I'm going to have to leave you again to tell the others what I've found. But that's not until the day after tomorrow. We have tonight and all day tomorrow to talk and play. Except for my morning walk. But it will be a short one, because I still want to go over all these papers before Saturday."

"Chirrup, cheep," was the answer.

AUGUST 7, 1993

Two days later

"I'M COFFEE'D OUT." Patty plopped onto a large, soft yellow chair, with three big patterned pillows behind her. "Everyone wanted to talk, and everyone wanted to talk while drinking coffee. Except for the women I met who drink at the Cecil. They had some surprising information for me. But they only drank beer."

They were all at Command Central. As usual, a fire was burning and Denise had plates of hors d'oeuvres on the coffee table. Denise shopped and cooked when she wasn't at her office counselling people. She loved to prepare special treats, especially when the women were as appreciative as this group. The women all helped themselves to drinks from the kitchen and then gathered around the fire, reaching for the veggie couscous and ricotta poppers, little balls of deliciousness.

Jo-Jo chewed on a popper. "My goodness, but this is good. Makes up for all that time tailing Swiftsure. But I do have some information."

They sat, silently chewing. Even Patty couldn't ask her usual barrage of questions, she was so busy filling her mouth.

After a few seconds silence while they finished chewing and swallowing, everyone started to talk at once.

"Whoa." Denise held her hands up, laughing. "Let's talk one at a time here. We'll start with the eldest."

She smiled at Fanny.

"Before I tell you what I found from my work in the library, I have to share with all of you something I came across quite serendipitously. I thought it was a little nugget of information you might appreciate. Our fact for the day: In 1874, the first athletic cup was used by men in sports. In 1974, men started wearing helmets for sports. What can we deduce from this? It took men one hundred years to realise their brains were as important as their genitals."

A burst of laughter filled the room.

"Now," said Fanny, turning serious, "let me tell you about this General."

"YOU'RE UNUSUALLY QUIET tonight, sweetie," Denise said later that night, when she and Noreen were getting ready for bed. "Something in particular bothering you?"

"Oh, I just wish we would have had that information on Sonderman when we went to see the president of the university."

"Really, don't even think about that. You know he wouldn't have believed you anyway."

"YOU JUST NEVER know what life holds, do you, Bunjie?" Fanny filled the little bird's container of special treat seeds. "I'm so glad that I knew how to hunt down information. And all the women tonight—they were so glad that I did. They really were, Bunjie. And then Merle—having that old friend who was still in the army. That didn't hurt us either, did it?"

"Cheepy, chirp," the little bird swung up and back on the swing. Fanny loved people, but she loved the times she shared with her bitty bird the most. She told Bunjie everything.

Fanny pulled a chair out from the table beside Bunjie's cage, and the little bird hopped up on the swing closest to Fanny.

"You know what Merle told us, Bunjie? One of her best friends actually had a run-in with that General. Merle told us all about meeting with Mavis." Fanny took Bunjie a decade back to an army office where Mavis was a sergeant working under General Sonderman.

"Sergeant, come into my office now."

"Sir." Mavis went into the General's office.

"Close the door, Sergeant."

"Yes sir," Mavis complied.

"So, what are your plans for tonight?"

"Sir?"

"How about you and me get together?" He winked at her. "You know what I mean, don't you?" He tapped his upper thigh.

"Sir, I'm sorry, I'm not able to do that."

"What's the matter, you one of those lezzies?"

"Sir, I'll go back to my desk now, sir."

"Hold on there, missy. What's the problem here? You don't want to make it with a General?"

"Sir, please, I'd like to go back to my desk now."

"And I'd like to take your clothes off and show you how a General does it. I could convince you not to be a lezzie anymore."

"I'm going now, sir."

"You are one of them. I knew it. Go then, you sick lezzie. Get the hell out of here," he yelled angrily. He stood up at his desk, and Mavis could barely open the door fast enough.

She later told Merle that the General's moods had changed so quickly, from polite, to friendly, to lecherous, to angry; she'd never seen anyone change emotions like that. He'd made a few comments earlier, but had never been quite so blatant.

Merle told the group that Mavis had reported the General, but nothing ever came of it, except that very shortly thereafter, she was transferred to another base.

"Whoever would have thought that someone in our army, the Canadian army, Bunjie, could be so crazy and so dangerous and no one could touch him. Hard to believe, isn't it? But it's true, Bunjie, it's really true."

AUGUST 11, 1993

Four days later

GENERAL SONDERMAN STUCK an unlit cigar in his mouth as the plane taxied down the runway. This island had been a smart move on his part. He remembered almost fifteen years ago, right after he was made General, how he tried to convince the others to turn this island into an army base. It could have so many potential uses, he argued for what seemed like years. Once they turned it over to him to "oversee", he was home free. And oversee that island he did, using it for his own devices for over a decade in between the training exercises and other activities he organized there for the army. He smiled. Life was good. Now, he had to get off the plane and deal with Clovis.

"I *WANNA* GO back," Clovis said. "Calgary is my home. My house is still there. My lab is still there."

The General was not pleased with Clovis. Frustrated, he sighed deeply. "The army is gonna give you a house and a lab. They all believe you're dead in Calgary. You don't need to go back there."

"Maybe I don't need to go back." Clovis shuffled his foot in the sand. "Maybe. But I want to. It's what I know. I did what you asked, General. I've completed the work you wanted. Now I need to go back where I belong."

"Look, Clovis," the General bit down on his cigar, which was now lit and stinking up the pristine air of the island, "don't say another word. We've settled things for you with our American colleagues. You are going to Washington, D.C. You'd be an unknown there. You can work in an army lab. We've arranged it all."

Clovis stamped his foot. "I'm not doing that. You never told me I had to do that. You never told me I had to go to Washington when you insisted I bring my passport with me. You told me I needed it for army regulations. You're the one who wanted to pretend I was dead. I never even wanted that. How will I be famous if I'm dead and no one knows I'm here?"

"I don't give a shit what you want," Sonderman said. "I want your work. You say it's completed. Fine. When you are finished with that work, I am finished with you. And you are going to the US of A. Whether you like it or not."

"I'm not!" cried out Clovis, like a petulant five year old. "I'm not going there."

"You are," shouted Sonderman, "and I don't wanna hear another word about it." He stormed up the hill and disappeared into a staff bungalow.

Clovis stood alone on the beach, wondering what he could do. He did not want to start another life. He had to keep reminding himself he was supposed to be dead, because he sure didn't feel that way. He never believed for a minute anyone would actually believe he was dead. He knew the General had told everyone he died in the fire, knew there was a memorial for him, but he didn't really believe it was going to affect his life. He had done all the lab work for the General. Now he longed for home. Home was Calgary, not some other place he didn't want to be. He was supposed to be famous. What was happening with that? He'd never be famous now, stuck in some army lab in another country.

AUGUST 12, 1993

Next day

THE ARMY PLANE came to a stop at the army base in Virginia, just outside Washington, D.C. Clovis was escorted to a black car waiting by the plane and driven into Bethesda, Maryland. As they drove through Bethesda, the driver pointed to a large building complex.

"In that group of buildings over there is the lab where you are going to work." He smiled at Clovis. "It's only a fifteen minute drive from your new home."

Clovis didn't respond. He didn't want a new lab. He didn't want a new home. He wanted his old one. He wanted *his* home. In Calgary. The soldier/driver stopped in front of a large, newly constructed building.

"Here's your temporary place." He smiled at Clovis.

They walked up to the apartment. It was nice enough, Clovis grudgingly admitted when he looked around.

"We'll get you a house soon, Doctor. For now, this apartment will have to do." The soldier put the keys down on a wooden sideboard near the front door. "We'll bring a car around for you later. Is there anything else you need right now?"

Clovis looked around at the new brown vinyl sofa and easy chairs, beige wall-to-wall carpets, tan non-descript walls, everything looking like it had never been used before and was neutral enough for anyone who might live there.

"No," he answered sullenly. He was not happy. Not in the least.

As soon as the soldier left, Clovis went to the window and looked out onto the street. Leaving the keys on the sideboard, he walked out the door, went down to the street, and hailed a taxi.

"To the airport, hurry," he instructed the driver.

"Which airport? There are three around here, you know."

"I don't care which airport. The closest one, okay."

"One airport, coming up." The driver wheeled around and headed onto the Beltway.

GENERAL SONDERMAN SAT in his office on the army base in Calgary and looked up when he heard a knock on the door.

"You have a phone call, sir. From Washington, D.C. It's someone from the US army; he says it's urgent."

Sonderman picked up the phone as the soldier quietly closed the door behind him.

"What d'ya mean, he's missing?" Sonderman yelled into the phone. "How could he possibly be missing?"

After he hung up the phone, he asked his aide to get Lester for him as quickly as possible.

AUGUST 13, 1993

Next day

WHEN CLOVIS ARRIVED in Calgary, he wasn't sure where to go. He thought someone else might be living in his house now; at least, that's what the General had told him. He couldn't just walk back into the university. They all thought he was dead. He didn't want a fuss and he didn't want the General to find him. That last talk with him, actually a shouting match, had scared him. He saw something in the General that was truly alarming, a violence just below the surface. He remembered how frightened he had been of him before. He sat down heavily on a blue chair in a long row of seats in the Calgary airport to figure out what to do now that he was finally back home.

JO-JO WAS JUST returning to Calgary from a visit to New York. She hated to leave Calgary for even a day, but her New York condominium finally sold and she had to deal with the details. She had decided to spend her life, at least her current life, in Calgary. She loved the area, loved going to the mountains, her mother was here, and she really enjoyed her new friends. She had a great job with a lock and safe company and recently had been certified as a professional locksmith. Finally, she could use her skills doing something legal. And it sure was an exciting time in Calgary, all of which made her very happy. She swung her carry-on over her shoulder and started to walk through the airport to the parking lot where she had left her car when she saw him. Her father taught her well. Always be on alert in public. Never do a double-take, never let on that you notice something, anything, take everything in, remember it all, and act as though you've seen nothing. She just casually kept walking through the terminal but she was certain that she had seen Clovis sitting on a bench there. She knew there was some suspicion that he wasn't really dead, and so thought she shouldn't be that surprised. But why would he show up in Calgary? That was pretty stupid. Then she remembered Noreen and Claire telling them all how brainless he really was, so she guessed it was believable.

It was late Friday afternoon and she was supposed to go to Command Central later that evening where all the rest were going to catch up with each other.

DENISE HAD JUST put the baked Brie with slices of baguette on the table in front of a roaring fire when Jo-Jo walked in. They had become so familiar with each other since this house became the center of their activities. Usually, people knocked or rang the bell, and then walked right in without waiting for an answer.

"Where's Nori," Jo-Jo asked urgently.

"In the other room. Hang on. Nooorrrii," she called. "Jo-Jo needs you." She turned to Jo-Jo. "How was New York? Good trip?"

"Yeah, but never mind New York. Guess who I saw at the airport?"

NOREEN AND DENISE, Claire and Patty, Fanny and Merle and Jo-Jo sat around the fire.

"Okay, Jo-Jo, tell 'em." Noreen shifted in her chair.

Jo-Jo repeated what she had told Noreen and Denise.

"I couldn't believe it was him, but then you said he was an imbecile, right? So I tailed him for a bit, but I have a feeling he's going to go to the university tonight. Why else would he come here? He wouldn't go into his house. He did drive by it though. But he just kept on going. I bet he's going to his lab on the third floor, to see it after the fire. If, in fact, there really was a fire," she added. "And I think we should see if we can surprise him there."

Everyone started to talk at once.

"Wait, wait," Denise said. "One at a time, please. I can't hear anything when you all talk at once."

Everyone was very excited. And every one of them wanted to check the third floor lab that evening and the next day and the next if they had to.

THE SEVEN WOMEN walked into the Science Building about nine-thirty that evening, well before the doors locked for the night. Since it was the start of a weekend, there was hardly anyone there. They went into Claire's and Noreen's office and left their jackets and purses there. They all agreed to take their cues from Jo-Jo, who knew about sneaking up on folks and such things. They walked up the stairs to the third floor, and Jo-Jo slowly opened the door, stuck her head out, and looked around. Nothing. She listened for a while. Nothing, but the smell of freshly worked wood and new office furniture. She waved them on, but put her finger to her lips. Fanny adjusted her purple beret with the feathers, and they tip-toed down the hall toward the main lab. None of the lights were on.

After the fire, the labs had been redesigned, and although they all had a main door, there were larger windows than before that one could see through while walking down the hall. Everything seemed very still and quiet. No one had moved back to the third floor yet.

Jo-Jo held her hand up. She pointed to her right. There, through the windows of the main lab, in the dark, a figure with long hair sat on a stool in the middle of the room. She wasn't sure who it was. She indicated the women should remain in the hall and she went forward. She pulled a gun from her jacket.

"A gun!" Merle whispered.

"Shhh," the others hissed.

Jo-Jo walked into the lab and flicked on the light. The figure started.

"Hello, are you here to work?" asked Jo-Jo.

"No, I'm uh, here to, um . . ." The person turned around. It was Clovis, wearing a very bad wig.

"Wherever did you get that wig, Dr. Clovis?" Jo-Jo asked, smiling.

"Wait, do I know you? Who are you? What d'you want?" Clovis got up and started walking towards the door.

Jo-Jo held out her arm. "I wouldn't do that if I were you." She indicated the gun.

Clovis froze. "Who are you? What d'ya want with me? I mean no harm. I'm not hurting anything. Lemme go."

"The only place you're going is into that hallway with me." Jo-Jo gestured with the gun.

"Not so fast, little lady." Jo-Jo and Clovis turned around. A soldier stood there, dressed in fatigues. He did not look overly friendly. He had very short hair, a long frightening scar down his face, and was brandishing a gun.

"I believe the good doctor will be coming with me. Now why don't you be a good little girl and sit down on that chair and stay there for ten minutes. That way, no one will get hurt." He looked at Clovis. "Well, almost no one." He leered.

"I'll take the gun though." He gestured to Jo-Jo.

She reluctantly handed him her gun. He took it, opened it, and burst out laughing. "It's not even loaded. You dames are something else."

"Well, *I* knew that," Jo-Jo muttered, "but he didn't."

"Come." The soldier motioned to Clovis. "Wig and all." He jerked his head to indicate that Clovis walk. He followed Clovis out of the lab.

Jo-Jo turned to look out the window of the lab just in time to see Noreen step out from behind a door and take a whopping swing with a large metal bucket. She heard the clunk as metal hit the soldier's head, and he disappeared from view.

Jo-Jo scampered into the hall and quickly tied the unconscious soldier's legs and hands together, just like roping and tying a calf at the Stampede. She threw her arms high into the air like the cowboys did and quietly uttered, "Yee-haw!

She was very pleased that Fanny and Merle had insisted on their bringing strong cords in case they had to tie someone up, as they had said.

Patty and Claire quickly grabbed Clovis, kicked his legs out from under him, and sat on him while Noreen tied his hands behind his back.

Fanny turned to Merle. "Good thing we brought enough cords

with us on this adventure, wasn't it, Merle?" They did a thumbs up, then turned to enjoy the action taking place in the hallway.

"Stanton, is that you? What the hell are you doing here?"

"I might ask you that same question, dead Dr. Clovis."

"Look, I just came here to think. I mean no harm."

"No harm!" Claire burst out. "First you pretend to be dead when you're clearly not, then we find you here sitting in the dark wearing this ridiculous wig. What are you up to, Cleve Clovis?"

"Christopher, you're here too. Oh God, I screwed up."

"Ya think?" asked Patty.

"Let's get out of here as fast as we can," Jo-Jo said. "We don't want to be around when pretty boy here wakes up."

Jo-Jo took time to recover her revolver from the pocket of the soldier.

Jo-Jo smiled as she held open the door to the stairwell. "Let's boogie," she urged. All the women hurried down the stairs and exited the building, Clovis in tow.

THE VAN WAS deadly silent on the way back to Command Central, as they were all deep in thought. They decided that since it was now late on a Friday night, they would keep Clovis with them until they figured out what to do with him.

THEY PUSHED CLOVIS, face down, hands tied tightly together in front, onto the sofa in the living room. Then everyone sat down.

Jo-Jo brandished her gun again.

"A gun?" Merle asked.

"Don't perseverate, Merle. It isn't loaded. Look." Jo-Jo showed Merle the empty chamber.

"I think we should tie his feet up first of all, so he doesn't get out of here. And then I think we should call the police," Merle said.

"The police. No, don't call the police, please. It's not my fault, really. It's the General. Honestly. It's not my fault." Clovis fidgeted under Noreen's weight, as she sat on him. Patty helped by joining her. There was no way they were going to let him get away now that they had him there.

"What's with the wig, Clovis?" Noreen asked as she got up from his back. "Being dead wasn't enough? Now you have to be dead and ridiculous?"

"C'mon, Stanton, help me out here, please."

"Help you out? You steal our lab, you steal our grant money, you pretend to be dead, you wear that stupid wig, and you want us to help you? You're even more feeble-minded than I thought." Noreen tied his ankles and began to pace the room in agitation.

"And," Patty bounced lightly on Clovis' bum, "you even decided to come back from the dead on Friday the 13th."

Everyone except Clovis laughed.

"Please, let me explain," he begged.

"Nori, maybe we should do that," Claire said. "Let's let him explain. I would love to know what kind of explanation he has for everything. Really."

"Yeah, I would too," added Jo-Jo, "and if we don't like it, we'll just add some bullets to this empty chamber."

"Oh my God, no, don't do that, please. Just lemme explain," he pleaded.

They agreed and decided to move him.

And so seven women and a man wearing a bad wig with his hands bound tightly before him, ankles bound and tied to a chair, all sat around the living room. Clovis felt his heart rate increase and his mouth become dry as he looked around the semi-circle at such strong, intensely focused women.

Jo-Jo leaned forward. "Now talk. And we'd better like what we hear." She patted his knee with her gun and smiled.

AUGUST 14, 1993

Next day

PHILLIP WEBER OPENED the door to his office at noon on a Saturday morning. He shook his head. He had no idea when he became President of the University of Calgary that he would be coming in to work on the weekend with such little notice for such an unbelievable reason. Especially a weekend as beautiful as this one, when he had plans to go hiking in the mountains. He almost didn't come. At first he had refused. But those women were incredibly persistent. And they kept insisting Cleve Clovis was with them. How was that even possible? He had been to his memorial service. He even gave the eulogy. He left the main door open and turned on the lights in the conference room and prepared to get ready. He greeted the Provost, who arrived shortly thereafter, and then the Chair of the Board appeared with the Chancellor of the university.

Within thirty minutes, they were all there except for the instigators of this meeting. The RCMP officers showed up; President Weber nodded to his brother David, who was Commissioner in charge of the Alberta Division of the RCMP. When his brother had called him much earlier that morning, David went over to his house right away to help him organize this meeting, bringing the RCMP Sergeants with him.

David had also asked the Army Base at Sarcee to send army lawyers, and they were followed by the university lawyers, most all of them grumbling about having to come out on such a fine Saturday. As they all arrived, Weber ushered them in and they all took seats around the table in the large conference room at the side of his main office.

Shortly thereafter, to his utter shock and surprise, in walked seven women with Cleve Clovis in the middle, hands still secured in front. From the cords around his wrists ran a longer cord, which Noreen held as she walked, somewhat akin to leading a sheep. Clovis had a very bad wig sitting crookedly on his head.

"Phillip." Claire greeted. "Thank you for coming down today. And all of you." She nodded at the people seated around the table. "David. Good to see you again. Thanks for coming." She had spoken with Phillip Weber weeks earlier and found out about his brother and was particularly pleased to see him there.

"As you can see, it was important." She nodded at Clovis.

"I do see," replied Weber. "Everyone you suggested I call is here now, so shall we get on with it?" He leaned back in his chair. "Now can you tell all of us exactly what is going on?"

"I think we'll let Cleve tell you first." Noreen yanked the cord and pushed Clovis into a seat and then sat down beside him, Jo-Jo on the other side, with her hand in her pocket where she had her gun.

Clovis was very tired and hungry. He hadn't eaten all day yesterday, except for a very bad snack on the plane. The women offered him food the night before, but his pride did not let him accept anything from them other than a bit of water for his dry mouth.

They told him to try to get some sleep on the sofa, that the next day would be a big day for him, but he couldn't sleep at all. Especially since they always had at least one of them guarding him all night. They never once let him out of their sight, except when he went into the small guest bathroom with one of the women always at the door. And they all insisted that he keep wearing that wig. He didn't know why he thought it might be a good idea yesterday. The wig, he thought, would protect him from being recognized, since no one would even think he would be in Calgary. That wig had not even come close to living up to his expectations. His hands hurt and he was very frightened. He didn't know what would happen now that everyone knew he was not dead. Then he had this thought that he tried to push away—maybe now he could become famous. They were all here to listen to him, weren't they? Not those girls. But him. Maybe there would even be reporters later, and he could be in the newspaper.

Noreen's elbow in his side brought him back to the present reality. "Talk."

Fanny adjusted her hat and smiled. She would have so much to tell Bunjie. Though she had just heard Clovis' story the night before, she was certainly not going to miss this second telling of it.

"I think we can untie him before he starts to talk, don't you think?" the President asked Noreen.

"Yeah, I guess so. With everybody here, he's not going anywhere."

Noreen started to untie the cords, but Jo-Jo just stepped up beside Clovis and with one quick swipe of her knife, his hands were freed. He rubbed his wrists, and mumbled, to no one in particular, "Thank you."

"And you can take off that ridiculous wig too, Cleve, please," the President added.

Clovis obliged. "They made me wear it."

"Only because that's how we found you," Noreen said. "Now tell them what you told us."

It was a little easier telling it the second time and it seemed to go quicker than the night before. He told them all about the genetic viruses and how the General had devised the entire plan with the fire and his apparent death. He related how Swiftsure just took over his old lab and had been meeting regularly with the General and reporting to him on the island. "Look, I had to leave Washington. I couldn't possibly stay there. I was scared of that General. Really scared. And I didn't have anywhere else to go. I know he is probably back in Calgary, but this is the only place I know. Please, Phillip, you have to protect me. He'll kill me if he gets a chance. I just know he would."

Clovis had tears in his eyes, and his voice was filled with panic and fear. There was silence while this new information was absorbed.

President Weber looked at Claire and then Noreen. "I should have known something was amiss when the General wanted to do that briefing after the fire. At first I said no, but then he insisted so vehemently, I just let him do it. And you two tried to warn me about him and I didn't listen. I'm sorry." He slowly shook his head.

"Well, you're listening now." Claire smiled gently at him.

"So *that's* why the General was there at the fire. He bullied his way in," Denise said thoughtfully.

Noreen turned to the people around the table. "But that's not all. Tell them what you found out, Fanny and Merle."

Fanny straightened her hat. "I used to work in library services." "And I did some research on General Sonderman. And Merle here . . ." She pointed to Merle. "Merle also has some information. I'll start and Merle can finish."

"First of all, I found out that General Sonderman was stationed on the East Coast for ten years. He wasn't always a general, of course. Technically, he's a Major-General, which means there are two other ranks of General above him, but no doubt you already know that." Fanny smiled around the table.

"He got promoted to general when he returned from overseas after he and his crew, actually," Fanny coughed slightly and adjusted her hat, "his crew mostly, saved six men who had been shot down. Six Canadian men, bravely brought back to safety. Apparently, Sonderman did not do anything in terms of the actual rescue, but took all of the credit since he was the ranking officer. He was made General shortly thereafter. There had been a few complaints about him before he was promoted, but they were all by women, and so were not followed up."

"What kind of complaints?" President Weber asked.

"Mostly complaints of a sexual and sexist nature. Apparently on at least three occasions he tried to push himself on women who were under his command. These three women did nothing at first, but then sometime after the last event, all three came forward. They were heard, but nothing was done to the General. Also, there were complaints lodged that the General did not follow up with promotions for women under his command. This is all on record, and the army stated they would deal with General Sonderman their own way, but no reprimand is in the records. It looks as if their own way was to do nothing, because nothing apparently happened." She sat back and looked at Merle.

"And there's even more. Merle." Noreen gestured to her.

Merle patted Fanny's forearm and sat forward. "And I have a very good personal friend who has been in the army for decades. She immediately knew all about General Sonderman. He is well known in the army for abusing women. No woman ever wanted to work with him. The women stopped reporting him because nothing ever happened except they were leaned on even worse by him. My friend told me that the General had just laughed when he was told he would be reported. 'By girls?' he apparently exclaimed. 'Who on earth is going to believe crazy broads? Certainly not this man's army.'" It seemed clear that he hated women and had refused to work with them. I think you get the picture. I needn't go on any more about that."

"Tell them the rest," Noreen pushed.

"Well, my friend told me that Sonderman could basically do whatever he wanted to do, because everyone was frightened of him. Even other officers. He would yell, pretend to know everything about anything, threaten others, and they all buckled. Apparently he's a very imposing guy—tall, strong, loud voice, and not afraid to intimidate anyone, which he evidently does with great regularity."

"There's a bit more," Fanny said, "but for now and for the sake of brevity, I think you get the idea. We're not at all surprised that Dr. Clovis here is frightened of him."

Patty leaned forward on the table. "I don't know if this is relevant or not, but I was talking to some women who frequent the Cecil."

"The Cecil. Isn't that a rubby-dub bar in the east end?" asked Weber.

"Well, yeah, sort of." Patty winced, knowing it was also one of the few places in the city that lesbians could hang out with impunity. "Anyway, these women said there were lots of rumours flying around the bar that a group of men who were regulars there were responsible for all the violence at the Take Back the Night March last year. And they're pretty sure the instigators were soldiers stationed at the Army Base off Sarcee Trail. Now, we don't know this for sure, but we think they could be associated with General Sonderman."

"Oh yeah, and you should probably know about the soldier last night," Jo-Jo added.

"Soldier?" the president asked.

"Yes," Noreen continued, and she told him how she had to hit him on the head to knock him out in order to keep Clovis for themselves.

There was stifled laughter in the room.

"Thanks Noreen. And thank you, all of you," President Weber said. "You have given us much to think about."

"Well, I hope you're certainly going to do much more than just think," Noreen burst out.

"Nori," Claire said. "Be quiet."

"Look," said Noreen much quieter this time. "We really want to know what you're going to do. We caught Clovis but we don't want to just let him go."

"Nobody will let him go." President Weber stretched out his arms. "Look, it's getting on. It's the weekend. Not much will happen now. Why don't we let the RCMP take Clovis with them, and the army will let us know Monday what they're going to do about General Sonderman. Is that acceptable to everyone here?"

"Wait. Why are the mounties taking him? What are the charges?" Claire asked.

"Not so much charges, as protective custody, Doctor," David Weber said. "You wouldn't want to let him go free or send him off with these army fellows here in case that General gets his hands on him, right?"

"Oh. Yeah. I guess you're right about that."

"Well, Cleve," Noreen smiled at him, "we're going to miss having you as a house guest. Sure you wouldn't like to stay with us?"

"I think I'll take my chances with the mounties," Clovis mumbled.

The RCMP officers nodded. The army officers nodded. The lawyers and the university officials all nodded. Noreen, Claire, and the other five women looked at one another, whispered to each other, and then nodded as well.

"Okay then," President Weber said. "I suggest we adjourn and we'll all talk about this again on Monday."

The RCMP officers led Clovis out of the room, leaving his wig on the table.

The men from the army whispered something to the President and then left.

The lawyers left. The Provost, Chair of the Board, and Chancellor left.

"You did good work, all of you," President Weber said. "I speak for the entire university when I say we are grateful for all you did."

"It's not over yet," Noreen said.

"Oh?"

"Well, what about this General? He's obviously some sort of psychopath. Where is he? Who else is he going to use? What about the genetic viruses he and Clovis developed? We can't just ignore him or those viruses." Noreen slapped the table.

"And we won't. We won't ignore him at all. I promise you that."

"And we should believe you why?"

"Noreen," Claire burst out. "For Pete's sake, give him a break. He came here on a weekend and organized all these other folks because we asked him to, he listened to us, he's helping us, and he only just now found out about all of this. For heaven's sake." She looked at President Weber. "Sorry. She didn't mean it."

"That's okay. I understand it's been a stressful time for everyone." President Weber stood up, followed by his brother. "Let's get outside and enjoy this beautiful day and talk again on Monday, okay? It's been quite the morning. Lots to think about."

The women nodded, and the men left the room.

The seven women sat there in silence. No one said a word. After a few minutes, they began to smile. When they were all smiling widely, they started to laugh. A lot. They laughed and laughed until tears ran down their faces. And when they were all laughed out, they got up, walked out of the room, and went home.

AUGUST 16, 1993

Two days later

GENERAL SONDERMAN WAS puzzled. Lester appeared to be missing. Clovis was missing. Something was definitely not right and he hoped that nothing had gone wrong. Except for that jerk Clovis, he thought. I wouldn't mind it in the least if he just disappeared from the world and we never saw or heard from him again. He paced in his office, door tightly closed. He needed to think.

"What an asshole," he growled. "Here I set up a whole new home for him, in a nice country, with a nice job, the works. I gave him the works. And how does the jerk thank me? He comes running home to mummy. He probably never even had a mummy. What a total idiot. I couldn't believe it when intelligence told me he returned to Calgary. Why would he wanna do that? He could bust this thing wide open. I'm not ready yet to let the others know about our plans. They're good plans, but for now, they're mine. *Mine!* And this Clovis just thinks he can sashay into Calgary with no consequence? I'll show him consequence."

He stopped pacing and sat down.

"Calm down Steve," he said. "No need to get flustered. We'll sort this all out. Compose yourself." He took a few deep breaths and sat back.

"General." A soldier opened the door after knocking and stuck his head into the room.

"What d'ya want?" he asked, none to friendly.

"General, you're going to have to come with us," the soldier said and stepped into the room. He was joined by a second soldier.

"Says who?"

"Sir," the soldier replied, "Lieutenant-General Osterman has asked us to bring you to his office."

"If General Osterman wants to see me, he can damn well ask

me himself. Now get the hell out of my office," he yelled, and stood up to his imposing six foot four height. "Now! And close the door after you!"

"Yes sir." Both soldiers retreated.

Outside the closed door of General Sonderman's office, the first soldier faced his cohort.

"Osterman said it might be difficult to bring him."

"So what d'we do now?"

"Nothing. Osterman said if we had trouble, not to engage with Sonderman. Just let Osterman know and he would deal with it."

AUGUST 19, 1993

Three days later

NOREEN AND CLAIRE were returning to their offices after having lunch with Doris. They had been anxious to tell her everything that had happened regarding the return of Clovis, and the three of them had a wonderful, laugh-filled lunch at their favourite Chinese restaurant.

They had just said good-bye to Doris and headed toward the Science Building when they saw President Weber walking by himself down the path, something that struck them as quite unusual.

"Phillip, we never see you walking alone in these parts. What are you up to?" Noreen asked as the three of them formed a small huddle on the sidewalk.

"Oh, I just had some business to take care of in the Science Building and I thought it would be a beautiful day for a walk outside."

"Well, you are right about that, Philip. It is a beautiful day, is it not? Not to make the day any less beautiful, but what's the news about that General? Anything? It's already been five days since we brought Clovis here.

"I had hoped to hear from someone by now," Weber grimaced.

"Why don't you call the army," Noreen suggested. "You know they won't tell us anything."

"All right," Weber had agreed. "I hope they are willing to talk to me."

"Well, why wouldn't they? As far as they know, you are the one who first told them about Sonderman. Like they didn't know about him before," she added sardonically.

WITHIN AN HOUR, the phone rang in Noreen's and Claire's office.

Noreen picked it up. "Dr. Stanton here. Can I help you?"

"It's me. Phillip. I spoke with someone from the army. He told me that General Sonderman seems to have vanished."

"That's totally ridiculous. How can a General in the army just vanish?"

"Well, he said he would get back to me. I'll let you know if I hear anything. Sorry I couldn't tell you more." And with that, he quickly hung up.

AUGUST 20, 1993

One day later

ONE WEEK HAD elapsed since that Saturday meeting in the President's office. Clovis was back in his old home, under surveillance. No one had been living there after all. Yet again, the General had lied to him. Clovis was still a major part of the investigation and was told not to go far. He didn't mind; he was very happy to be back in his own home, with his own TV, his own remote, his own kitchen. He was happy to be in his own bed in his own bedroom and loved his own bathroom too. He was thrilled to just walk from room to room, smiling and not doing much of anything else.

He was anxious to get to the end of this saga. He had been contacted by a reporter, several reporters in fact, and a TV station, but the RCMP had instructed him not to talk to anyone at all until everything was completely resolved, including finding the General. This had disappointed him greatly. He was ready to talk, and certainly ready to be featured in the media. After all, it was his work that the General wanted, his, not those two girls, and he and his lab had produced it. When he spoke with the reporters, he thought he would leave out the part about the mistakes and the accidents. They could believe that it was all his brilliant scientific mind that had produced those viruses and no one had to know any differently.

Nothing had been heard from General Sonderman, which pleased him immensely, in spite of the fact he was anxious to go public. He knew the RCMP were watching his home in case contact was made by the General or any of his men. Clovis knew he would be very happy to stay in this house of which he was truly fond, under the watchful eyes of the RCMP, doing nothing but adjusting to being back in his home in Calgary.

AUGUST 21, 1993

Next day

THE SEVEN WOMEN once more were about to embark on an evening of gustatory delight, creative conversation, and just plain enjoyment, especially now after the past event-filled week. For the past eight months, they began sharing meals every few weeks or so. Aside from being comrades-in-arms, as Fanny described them, they all very much enjoyed each others' company.

"You know," Noreen looked around at her friends, "this is the first time in almost a year that we don't have to talk about you-know-who or make strategic plans. I suggest we do something entirely different tonight. To celebrate."

"Excellent idea, Nori. How about a game?" Denise asked.

"What game?" asked Claire.

"Let's invent one," suggested Patty. And they did.

As they were enjoying cocktails and hors d'oeuvres seated in the living room in front of the felicitous fire, they played the game they had just invented—What was the neatest thing you've ever done? They went around the room and each woman briefly told what she thought was the "neatest" thing she ever did or that ever happened to her. In her life.

"So far," Patty clarified. "The neatest thing that has happened to us in our lives, so far."

"Obviously." Claire smiled.

The women began to share their experiences.

"Okay, Jo-Jo. Your turn." Patty pointed at Jo-Jo with her fork.

The others sat up to listen more attentively. Since Jo-Jo was the neophyte in their group, they still didn't know very much about her history.

"Well," Jo-Jo started, "I don't believe I even need to think about what to tell you, it's so obviously the very neatest thing. So, the neatest thing I ever did was . . ."

About five years previously, there had been a series of violent rapes in the area of New York where Jo-Jo lived. At the time, she belonged to a feminist organization much like SWAC or ASWAC. As the number of rapes increased, the women in her group got together and decided that since the police weren't arresting anyone, they would have to take matters into their own hands. The very last rape had involved a woman many of them knew through their feminist connections. She had described the man to them, but she didn't know his name. She had given the police a very detailed description of her attacker, but so far, no one had been arrested.

Jo-Jo's group developed their own plan. They didn't want to hurt anyone; they would be acting against their own beliefs if they did that, but they did want to stop that man from raping anyone else. Since the police obviously knew about him and hadn't arrested him or anyone else, it was up to them to inhibit him from harming another woman. It wasn't hard to identify him from all the available information.

One night, in the early morning hours, thirteen women gathered outside the rapist's apartment. They were dressed in jeans, t-shirts, boots, no disguises at all, and they broke into his apartment building (with a little help from Jo-Jo). They quietly walked to the door of his flat. One of them had been watching earlier to ensure he was at home.

Jo-Jo opened the front door to the apartment and the women quickly and quietly walked into his bedroom and surrounded the bed. They stood very close together around three sides of the mattress, the fourth side being up against the wall. They didn't touch him or his bed. No one said a word. They stood there quietly with their arms at their sides, staring at him.

"What th' . . . ? Who the hell are you broads? Geddoud a'here! I'm callin' the police!"

The women stood there, very close, almost but not quite touching the bed, staring at this man who had hurt so many women. They didn't move. They didn't speak. They were almost shoulder to shoulder, impenetrable and impermeable. If he tried to get out of bed, he would have to go through them. And the look they all had was not very conducive to a safe and friendly passage.

"What d'ya want? What're ya doing here?" His voice was not as loud this time. "Who are ya? What're ya doing?"

The women stood there, almost touching each other, not moving, staring intently at the rapist.

"Get out." This time it was almost a whisper. Again, they didn't speak; they didn't move.

He started shaking. "What? Ya want money? What d'ya want? I'll give you what ya want. Just get out."

The women all remained silent, calm, and at rest.

The shaking got worse. Jo-Jo noticed a yellow stain spreading across the sheet.

"Please, leave me alone. Get out, please." The man shook with fear.

The women stood unmoving, unspeaking for half an hour, staring at the rapist. Soon they could smell his feces in the bed. After twenty minutes, he just lay shaking in that bed, terrified for his life.

Jo-Jo, who had been selected by the group to do this, broke the silence at the designated time.

"If you ever, ever hurt another woman again, we will know, and we will come here," Jo-Jo quietly and calmly said, while the other women stared at him, not moving. "The next time, we won't just stand around you. You understand?"

"Y-y-y-yes, ma'am," he stuttered.

"Understand?" Jo-Jo asked again.

"Yes, ma'am, I-I-I-I understand."

"Tell us you won't ever hurt another woman again. And mean it."

"Yes, ma'am, I won't ever hurt another woman again."

"Because if you do," Jo-Jo said, "you understand you won't live to see the next day."

"Yes, ma'am, I understand. I won't ever hurt another woman."

"Good."

And with that, the thirteen women turned and slowly walked out of the bedroom, leaving the rapist sitting in a pool of his pee and shit and fear.

They walked quietly and deliberately out of the apartment,

down the street, and when they turned the corner, they all talked excitedly at the same time. They were sure their plan had worked. And they were right. There were no more rapes by that man as far as they could tell. They thought they would like to do that again, for other rapists. And maybe they would. Jo-Jo had left New York very shortly after that. She still kept in touch with those women, but less and less as time went on.

"Wow," Patty exclaimed. "What a story."

"That was indeed pretty neat," Merle said.

"That was a wonderful story," Fanny offered.

AFTER THE COLD gazpacho, which was more delicious than usual because all the vegetables had just been picked hours earlier from Denise's own garden, they talked about Clovis and the General.

"I actually feel sorry for Cleve now," Claire said.

"Sorry for him. C'mon, he's a total jerk. How can you possibly feel sorry for him?" Noreen sat across the table from Claire and grabbed a piece of baguette, buttered it, and popped it into her mouth.

"Well, he's pretty incapable of even being a bad guy. I bet he just missed his home and his TV."

"I tend to agree with you, Claire. I think he's just an ineffectual guy who got caught up in something much bigger than he was and once the General got his hooks into him, he was sunk." Jo-Jo took a sip of wine.

"You know," Denise said, "I've just been reading about this newly defined syndrome, Asperger's, and I'm thinking that Clovis might be one of the folks who has it."

"Asparagus Syndrome?" Patty asked. "What the hell is that?"

"Not asparagus, Patty, As-per-ger," Denise said. "It's a developmental disorder, a syndrome considered to be a very mild part of the autism spectrum disorder, a high-functioning ASD. People with that have normal intelligence or even higher IQs than average but they aren't able to have normal social interactions, like empathy for others. And they can't form friendships. They're not able to share things with others. Oh, and they also have what's called impaired non-verbal behaviour, like they don't usually make eye contact, things like that."

"That would be our boy," said Noreen.

"These people just don't seem to tune in to others the way most people do," Denise continued. "They're just not aware of the feelings of the people around them. They're usually considered insensitive and socially awkward."

"That does seem to describe Cleve," said Claire. "Asperger Syndrome, you say?"

"Yeah. I think it's just becoming a diagnosis now, although autism has been around for a while. I was reading about it in one of my journals. I thought it might apply to Clovis. Something interesting I read about these people with Asperger's," Denise continued, "is that they often do very intense work in one particular topic, with lots of very detailed information, without really understanding the subject as a whole. That might explain why Clovis was able to do what he did."

"That's very interesting indeed," said Fanny. "It always helps to know why people do the things they do. Thank you for telling us about it."

"So what about all his Sir Toby work? That wasn't ineffectual," Patty managed to say in between bites. "What happened to that?"

"Not Sir Toby, Patty. I keep telling you, Sertoli. Sertoli cells." Claire smiled at her. "Well, we heard that the army has closed down that lab, and everything in it is going to be evidence, I guess. So right now, nothing has happened to it. All the viruses are still there, but no one has access to them, presumably, except some committee consisting of people from the army and the university."

"Say, where is that General now, anyway?" Patty asked.

"We have no idea," Claire answered. "What did Phillip tell you, Noreen? That the General . . . what again?"

"Well, according to Phillip, who spoke with someone, don't know who, in the army, the General has apparently," and here she made quotation marks with her fingers, "vanished."

"Oh, come on." Patty groaned. "That's ridiculous."

"Not really, when you think about it," Merle said. She put down her glass. "He must have known we were on to him, especially after you so nicely bested his soldier."

They all laughed.

"That was pretty good, wasn't it?" Noreen chuckled. "We had a good time tying up that soldier, didn't we?"

They all laughed again.

"You know, I might have an idea about the General," Fanny piped up.

"Do tell." Patty extended her arm out, palm up, indicating that Fanny should continue.

"Well, you know Clovis talked about being on that island. And according to him, there weren't many people on it. It seemed as though it was the General's island. Maybe that's where he ran to."

"Fanny, what a brilliant thought." Claire beamed at her.

'Yeah, great thinking." Denise started clearing the soup bowls.

"Where exactly is that island, anyway?"

"Clovis said he didn't know, remember, because they flew there."

They all burst out laughing again.

"He really is kind of stupid, isn't he?"

"He did say it was about five hours in the plane though, but who knows what kind of plane or how fast it went. But if he did go there, how could the army not know?"

'Well, either they really don't know, or—"

"They're not saying. Which one of those is it?"

"I'll call Phillip on Monday morning and ask him to call the army again. He can figure out what to say or ask about that island. Now that I think about it, it's a pretty good bet that's where that General is." Noreen looked to Claire who nodded her approval.

The rest of the dinner was delightful. Patty had recently returned from the Michigan Womyn's Music Festival and had many interesting tales to tell about the Festival. Everyone was anxious to hear all the stories about thousands of women camping in the woods, building stages for wonderful entertainment.

"Guess how much garlic you need to make enough Nutloaf to feed seven thousand hungry women?" Patty asked. "Thirteen pounds. Minced. And that's only one of about sixteen ingredients. Four hundred pounds of rice, a little more onions . . . Ah, but never mind all that food. You know what happened at the Night Stage?" she asked excitedly.

Clovis and the General did not make another entrance into the conversation that evening.

SEPTEMBER 2, 1993

Twelve days later

FOR YEARS, GENERAL Sonderman always made sure there were soldiers working and living on the island and always rotated them every few months to keep them on their toes. He used the island just enough for army business, such as training exercises, conferences, and the like to avoid suspicion of his other uses. The army had instructed him to oversee the island and trusted him to do so effectively. He chuckled to himself at their sissy trusting natures. He had found many excellent uses for the island to suit his own purposes over the years.

It was not unusual for him to pop in and check up on things as he usually kept either prisoners or other people with whom he worked on the island. What was unusual: his staying longer than a day or two. The reason for this was that the army truly had no idea what he did in these instances. Had they known, he felt they would not approve, but that's only because they couldn't see the whole picture. He had his Special Forces, loyal to him beyond doubt.

By the fifth day, the staff started thinking the General might be there for a while. To a man, they were frightened of him yet wanted his approval.

Every morning, the General arose in the hut he claimed for his own. He dressed in full army uniform despite the warm weather on the island. His staff organized an office for him, and he sat behind a desk doing "work" as he said. No one on the island had any idea what he did. He showed up regularly for meals, and it seemed as though he did not really socialize. Until the third week.

SAM, THE ISLAND chef, had just finished cleaning up after dinner. He enjoyed being on the island for a short period of time. Living here was different, peaceful, calm. He had most of what he needed to make good meals, and was pleased with the obvious enjoyment by the men of his culinary creations. He knew he was well liked by pretty much everyone. This three month rotation would be over in two more weeks, and because of the difference of this place from standard army bases, he would have stories to tell for years. There was plenty of time for the beach, swimming, reading, and experimenting with new dishes. All in all, he felt happy to be here—even with the General, who was not the easiest person to be around.

He swept his white cooking cap off his blond brush cut and sat down on a long bench by the table where the men sat. There were two other smaller tables for officers, but most officers sat with the men. Not this General though. He preferred to sit by himself. Well, mused Sam, that's his choice.

Just then, the door to the mess opened and slammed against the wall.

"Oops," someone said.

Sam turned to see General Sonderman leaning against the door, not looking at all as he normally did.

"Can I help you, General?"

"Yam Ses. Oops, I mean, yes, Sam." The General laughed.

Actually, it sounded more like a giggle. Coming from such a large man, it seemed totally incongruous.

"D'ya have anything to drink here? I wanna bottle of something."

"A bottle of what, sir?"

"A bottle of booze, you idiot," he boomed.

"Yes, I know sir, but what kind of booze?"

"Whatever you have," he yelled again.

"Yes sir. I'll get something for you."

Sam went into the storeroom and brought out a bottle of scotch. He thought the General might be a scotch man.

"Here you go, sir. Is there anything else I can do for you?" Sam immediately regretted asking.

"Sure, Sam. Sit down. Have a drink. Maybe you can bring some snacks, too."

Sam set two glasses and some chips on the square table and

indicated with his hand for the General to sit, which seemed redundant to Sam since the man did whatever he wanted anyway.

General Sonderman more or less fell into the chair.

"Sir," Sam took a deep breath in, "can I get you a coffee, sir?"

"No, you idiot, you cannot. No coffee, Sam, Goddammit. Sit. Drink," the General ordered.

They sat in silence for the first few minutes. The General finished his glass of scotch before Sam had even taken his second sip. He held his glass out to Sam for a refill.

"Sir, is something wrong?" Sam tentatively asked.

"Wrong. Why would you think something is wrong? Fill this glass up again, soldier."

"Yes sir. Well, it seems, sir, as though you're drinking a bit more than usual, sir."

Sam wondered what the situation might have been like off the island. He knew that back in Canada, he could never have addressed the General like this. The relationship between officers and grunts, as they were often called, was much more informal here. That was another reason why so many of the soldiers liked it here; also the relatively easy work, peaceful existence, almost like being on a holiday.

"Yes. Drinking," said the General. "Drinking, dranking, drunk." And with that, his head crashed down on the table.

Sam sat there for a few minutes determining what to do. He'd seen his share of drunk soldiers, but this was different. A ranking officer sat here, one who terrified everyone, passed out at his table in the mess. If Sam left him here, the General would feel terrible in the morning and blame Sam. If Sam took him to his cabin, the General might accuse Sam of moving him. If Sam called someone else, the General would be angry at Sam for involving others. It wasn't looking too good for Sam.

LESTER HAD TO think seriously about recent events. He knew the General was displeased with him because he lost Clovis, and yet, he had insisted he come with him to this island of his.

Lester had been here many times over the years, but never for more than a few days at a time. Now, once they returned to Canada, if that idiot Clovis talked to the army or the police, he felt certain the General would be court-martialed and Lester likely would be court-martialed alongside him. The General had promised to protect him, but Lester doubted that he could live up to that promise.

When Lester had regained consciousness lying hog-tied in the hall of the Science Building, he had to think about what he was going to tell the General. He certainly couldn't tell him that he had been bested by girls who stole Clovis from him. In the early hours of the morning, a flashlight shone upon his face.

"What's happening here?" a tall, black-haired security guard knelt over him. He pulled the handkerchief out of his mouth.

"Thanks," Lester gruffly mumbled.

Leo undid the ropes while Lester told him about some students ambushing him and tying him up on a dare.

"I wouldn't do anything about it." he smiled at Leo. "They were just students acting out. They didn't mean any harm. As you can see, I'm perfectly fine."

Leo was fairly adamant about wanting to report the incident, but Lester had repeatedly asked him not to, to just let boys be boys, it didn't mean anything at all, they knew that Leo would come up there on his rounds, and he, Lester, had only been there for a very short time. Not entirely true, as he left out the hours he was unconscious, but Leo did not need to know about that.

When Lester left the university, he did not go straight back to the army base. Instead, he went to the Cecil Hotel where he got a room and lay in bed for two days, resting and thinking before he showed up with a story he thought the General would buy. He would be angry enough about having lost Clovis; he didn't need to be angry at Lester for anything more.

Yet he still felt a strong loyalty to the man who found Lester overseas, scarred from battle, and helped him heal. The General even made him head of his Special Forces. These special forces were not *really* special forces, Lester knew that. They belonged solely to the General, not to the Army. Yet the men in these Special Forces all loved the General and were dedicated to him.

Lester lay on his cot, arms behind his head, reminiscing. A

picture of the bar inside the Cecil Hotel in Calgary popped into his head. A few years ago, the General ordered his Special Forces to infiltrate a group of men who regularly hung out at the Cecil. Lester and a few others of the General's cadre all started drinking beer with Big Bo and Jinky and their group of men, always talking about three of their favourite topics: sports, how Lester got the scar that ran from his left eye down to his chin, and how much they hated girls. Or women, as they now liked to be called. They all hated them, at least, what they were becoming now that a new century was almost upon them. The men all liked sex with females, that was certain, as long as the women knew their place. Barefoot, pregnant, and in the kitchen, they would say. Not these modern ladies, who were like another species, who felt they belonged in a man's world, but were so wrong. If they only knew how wrong they were.

One night about a year earlier, Lester suggested, as the General told him to do, that they all go down to the upcoming Take Back the Night March and do some serious damage. That was all he had to do. Then he just sat back and watched it happen. The men did all the rest. Lester didn't mean for any people to actually die. None of the men would admit to taking that first shot. He didn't think anyone would actually bring guns. He had to admit that things did get a bit out of hand. Even the General was not too pleased with the final outcome of that March. For the upcoming March, the men had all decided to stay away.

"I'm not going near any of those gun-toting broads no more," Jinky had said.

"Me neither. Last year was too intense." Big Bo swigged his beer.

After a while, Lester and his two compatriots had stopped going to drink beer with the men. The General decided to leave that plan for a while. He had something new he was working on. This genetic thing.

And now, almost a full year after that March, Lester found himself on the island with the General waiting for God knows what. Waiting. He hoped the General would think them out of this one.

A KNOCK ON his cabin door brought Lester out of his reveries. "Enter."

"Lester, you have to help me." Sam the cook stood at the door.

Lester sat up on his cot.

"The General, he's passed out drunk in the mess. I don't know what to do with him."

Lester sighed. "Leave it to me." He was used to dealing with things. Especially things that had to do with the General, one way or the other.

Sam uttered a huge sigh of relief. "Thanks, Lester. You're a lifesaver."

"I'll deal with it, I said. Now go do whatever it is you do." Lester brusquely walked by him, out the door, and headed toward the mess.

SEPTEMBER 3, 1993

Next day

NOREEN AND CLAIRE walked into President Weber's office.
"Well, Phillip, what's the latest from the army?" Noreen asked.
"And hello to you too, Noreen." He smiled at her.
"Hi, Phillip, have you spoken with them yet?" Claire asked.
"In fact, I just got off the phone with Lieutenant-General Osterman. I spoke with him earlier and told him your theory—that the General could be on that island. You girls," he smiled sheepishly, "I mean you women, were right again. That's where he is. And they are working on a plan to extract him, in army talk."
"Extract him? Sounds like the work we do in the lab." Noreen laughed.
"Well, at any rate, it's all happening, and soon the General will be court-martialed, and Clovis is going to have to testify, and they may even need to call on you girls. Umm, women."
Noreen and Claire had to admit that he was at least trying.
"Say, how about relocating our lab to the third floor. Those new renovations after the fire are pretty cool, and we think we'd like to be back there," Noreen said as Claire nodded. "Since the initial move came from this office, the Head of the Science Department says we can't move back unless you approve it. The labs are brand new and Clovis' old lab hasn't moved back there yet."
"I guess we owe you that." President Weber smiled.
"Cleve can go to the first floor, if he wants to come back." Noreen laughed.

SEPT 18, 1993

Two weeks later

EXCERPT FROM THE Calgary Courier:

The Take Back the Night March took place last night, starting at City Hall and winding down 11th Ave SW. The March was considered successful and peaceful. Last year's March resulted in three dead and seven seriously injured after violence broke out along the route. There were no charges by police for last year's March.

This year, there was no repeat of any violence. The organizers were pleased with the outcome. Mary Kirsten, chairwoman of Alberta Status of Women Action Committee (ASWAC) and on the board of Calgary Status of Women commented: "We were very pleased with the March this year. There was no violence of any kind. It's true, the numbers were down somewhat, but we hope now the city can see that violence isn't a given for the March, and more people will attend next year."

The Take Back the Night Marches occur each year on the third Friday of September.

SEPTEMBER 19, 1993

Next day

THE GENERAL HAD made a significant dent in Sam's scotch supply over the past ten days. Sam only had a few more days left on his tour on the island, and had ordered extra scotch along with the other supplies that would be needed for his replacement. Three months—it had been a good time for Sam, even the last few weeks with the General drinking all his supplies.

Lester heard the plane before he saw it. It was just a matter of time until they came for the General. He knew what he had to do. He had to take care of the General just the way the General had taken care of him. He quickly ran to the landing strip to talk to the man in command of these new arrivals to their island.

The General heard the knock on the door and put his hung-over head in his hands. Damn planes. Damn noise.

"What?" he yelled at the door.

"It's, Lester, sir. Can I come in?"

"Lester! Why didn't you say so. Come."

"Sir, they've come for us. We have to go with them now."

"What're you talking about? Go where?"

"Sir, General Osterman has ordered his men to bring us back to Calgary."

"That's ridiculous. Where's that little boat we hid? Let's hop in that boat. They 'll never find us." He stood up and walked to the door.

"Sir, remember when we were at Altray? We were young and strong and we could do anything. That was almost twenty years ago. A lot of time has passed since then. The soldiers that came today are just like we used to be. We can't beat them."

"You're sure of that?"

"Sir, they're all around this cabin. We can't go anywhere. It's over, sir. We have to go back with them."

The General sat down heavily on the cot beside Lester. "Over?" he asked, somewhat quietly.

"Sir, perhaps if you just go back and spell out to them what you were doing with the genetics project. Perhaps you'll be seen as a forward thinking hero. If you could just explain to them . . ."

"Maybe. Maybe you're right. What do you mean they're around this cabin?"

Lester looked sadly at the General. "I told them I would bring you out, Sir. They have come to take you back." He placed his hand gently and tentatively on the General's shoulder. It was not shrugged off.

Lester thought about how he had to think quickly and talk fast to the new soldiers on the island. He stood at the bottom of the stairs to the plane and asked to talk to the man in charge. He told him that he would be able to bring the General to them and would save everyone a lot of unpleasantness. He practically begged for just fifteen minutes with the General and he would bring him to the plane. They were only too happy to oblige. He was glad he did that. He would hate to see what would have happened had he not been there to act as a buffer between the General and the rest of the army.

Lester hoped they could be put in the brig together. He wanted to take care of the old man. God knows the General had taken care of Lester when it mattered. Now it was Lester's turn. He owed him at least that much and he intended to make good on that debt.

"It's time to go now, Sir. They're going to take us back to Calgary. I'm coming with you, Sir. Everything will be fine. I think you just need to clarify to General Osterman and the others back home exactly what you were doing. You'll be fine. Come, Sir." He stood up and waited for the General. They both walked to the door together.

"Ready?" Lester asked.

The General tucked his shirt in neater, shrugged, straightened his shoulders, and nodded.

"Okay, then." Lester opened the door wide.

Sam looked out the door of the mess hall. He hadn't been told all these soldiers were coming, and he wondered how long they would be there. He wasn't sure he would have enough to feed them all for lunch. No one had notified him. The radio room was just off the mess and Sam was in there that very morning to order more supplies. No one told him they were having guests.

He saw two lines of soldiers, ten to a row, on either side of the footpath to the General's cabin. They just stood there, quietly, not doing anything. Then he saw the door of the cabin open. The General appeared, and Lester was right behind him. As the General, with Lester following closely, started to walk down the pathway, the soldiers all stood at attention and saluted. They walked in silence through two lines of saluting soldiers who then fell in right behind them. They walked right up to and into the waiting plane.

SEPTEMBER 28, 1993

Nine days later

EXCERPT FROM THE Calgary Courier:
The Canadian Armed Forces, Calgary Sarcee Trail Base, has confirmed the impending court-martial of Major-General Steven Sonderman. General Sonderman was arrested earlier this month on an unnamed island in the Pacific and was returned to the Calgary base, where he had been stationed. This arrest and impending court-martial occur the same month as the Take Back The Night March. Last year at the March, fighting erupted between the men and women, resulting in three fatalities and numerous serious injuries. An army spokesman has just confirmed that General Sonderman was responsible for instigating the violence last year and an apology to the women of Calgary will be forthcoming. This year, The Take Back the Night March which took place ten days ago was peaceful and considered successful.

General Sonderman has been charged with involvement with illegal genetic engineering as well as indirectly causing three deaths and multiple injuries at last year's Take Back The Night March. Other charges being considered are failure to consider promotions for any females under his command and improper advances to women under his command.

Along with General Sonderman, six other soldiers are being court-martialed, all of them being a part of the General's "Special Forces" and were the ones who carried out his commands. The court-martial proceedings are not expected to be completed until next month. The Army spokesman was not prepared to comment on the court-martial at this time, but said that a full statement will be given once the legal proceedings have been completed.

SEPTEMBER 29, 1993

Next day

"WHY DID HE say we're having a meeting?" asked Patty as the seven women headed up to the President's office.

"I dunno. He just called and said he wanted to talk to all of us, everyone who was at the initial meeting that Saturday. He asked me if I'd organize the women and I said sure." Noreen held the door open for them.

"And here we all are." Fanny smiled.

"And here we all are." Merle smiled back.

"COME IN, COME in." President Weber held his arm out, indicating they should all go into the conference room where they initially met more than five weeks earlier. "Come in, take a seat, all of you."

The women walked into the room and looked around. There were more than half-a-dozen people already sitting there.

Weber introduced them. "This is the Chancellor of the university, whom you've already met, the Provost, the Registrar, Dean of Graduate Students, the Dean of Arts and Science, the Head of the Science Department . . ."

The women sat down in seats at one end of table.

"We asked all of you here today because we wanted to officially offer our deepest gratitude to each of you for your part in this whole affair with Clovis and the army," President Weber said. "Without your help, the university, in fact the whole city and more, would have been in deep trouble. We did get information that your initial instincts were correct; that the General was in fact responsible for instigating that terrible violence at the Take Back the Night March last year. As I'm sure you all know, this year's March was very successful. Peaceful, even if the numbers were down. People will start coming back now that they know the violence isn't a given. We wanted to let you know everything we heard from the Army and RCMP, answer any questions you may have, and mostly, say a big thank you to each of you women for doing everything you have done this past year."

He looked at Noreen and Claire, then gazed at Jo-Jo and grinned. "Well, maybe not breaking into the labs, but pretty much everything else."

"Would you have believed us, Phillip, if we had told you what we thought?" Noreen asked.

"Good point. Probably not. For those who don't know, Noreen and Claire did come to see me, trying to tell me about General Sonderman. Unfortunately, I did not see the truth in their words at that time. I've learned to listen harder now. And I will.

"Okay, let me just finish up with some information. After Noreen called me to tell me that the General was probably on some island—"

"That was Fanny's idea, actually," Noreen said.

"Thank you, Fanny, for that." President Weber smiled at the septuagenarian. "General Sonderman was arrested on that island and brought back to Calgary where he is currently in the brig, awaiting court martial. Dr. Clovis will have to testify. The prosecutor still was not sure whether they were going to charge him or not in civil court. He seems to want to wait until after the court-martial which I gather will be expedited and happen quickly. That soldier that you knocked out, Noreen, apparently his name is Lester Southern. He and five others will all be court-martialed along with the General. I think some of them have made deals with the army. They told authorities what they did at the Cecil bar—how, at the General's behest, they were to rile up the men for the Take Back the Night March and other events in the city where mostly women were present. At any rate, the army is dealing with all of that. The RCMP have referred Dr. Clovis to the provincial prosecutor. Dr. Clovis has indicated that he would like to come back to work here. His request is under consideration, pending outcome of other investigations. I think that pretty much sums things up, doesn't it? Have I left anything out?"

"Don't think so, Phillip," Noreen said. "Thanks so much for all this."

"You're very welcome. Now I think the Chancellor wants to say a few words. Chancellor?"

After all the bigwigs said their piece and thanked the women for their participation and bravery, a staff aide brought in some champagne and some hors d'oeuvres. Everyone stood up and mingled so that those from the university had a chance to speak with each of the women.

Fanny adjusted her hat and smiled. She would have so much to tell Bunjie when she returned home. She very much enjoyed watching everyone but was not quite as loquacious as Merle, who thrived in circumstances such as these.

At one point, Patty leaned over to Denise, winked and whispered, "Pretty classy, but nowhere near as delicious as your goodies."

Each of the women were pleased to be at the event and were all quite touched that President Weber had organized this thank-you gathering.

SEPTEMBER 24, 1994

One year later

THEY STILL REFERRED to the house as Command Central, even though it had been a year since the end of the "Clovis Incident" and The Y Syndrome. They all got together and eagerly anticipated Denise's gustatory treats. She had made caviar pie again, because she knew it was one of their favourites. Denise hummed as she got all the appetizers ready in the kitchen. She was happy because lately Noreen was happy. Noreen and Claire had recently discovered something important in their field; Denise didn't quite understand the finer points of all of it, but she was thrilled that Noreen and the whole university, had been pleased with their work.

Since the whole Clovis Incident, the seven women got together at least once a month. They had talked over the whole thing *ad naseum*, Denise had thought, but as a therapist, she realized that talking and talking and talking was important in coming to terms with crises.

She walked into the living room, carrying a tray of wonderfully looking food.

Patty jumped up. "Ooooh, how good is this." She took a cracker, dipped it into the caviar pie, and stuck it in her mouth.

"Hey, Patty," Denise sat on the arm of the sofa, "I heard that the Monument is actually going to happen now. Is that true?"

"Yep, it sure is. Finally. After several years we've finally agreed on this thing. It's actually going to happen. It'll be unveiled early in the spring. At long last, a monument for women who were victims of male violence."

"That's very good," Merle added. "You did a good job with that, Patty."

"Well, we just needed to persist with it. Just like The Dinner Party. Remember all that?"

The women explained to Jo-Jo that in the early '80s, they had wanted to bring Judy Chicago's Dinner Party to the Glenbow Museum. They met with the director who immediately said no. When they asked why, he thought for a bit, and then said that they didn't have a space big enough for the exhibit. One of the women in their group who worked at the Glenbow got ahold of the architectural plans and discovered a wall that was not weight-bearing and could be removed. They went back to the director. He then said:

"Well, okay," he said, "we have the space, but we will lose money on it. You have to put up a guarantee of ten thousand dollars."

"But the Egyptian exhibit that was just here didn't have to do that," Patty mentioned.

"Well, we're not taking the chance on this. Sorry. Looks like you can't have it here."

That was a Friday afternoon. The following Monday at nine a.m., the group of women were in his office with ten thousand dollars.

"The community really wants this."

He capitulated.

"And the thing was," Merle explained. "It was one of the most successful exhibits ever held at the Glenbow and made more money for them than any other exhibit."

"And we learned so much," said Fanny. "I didn't really know the names of women pirates before."

"It was wonderful," Jo-Jo said. "I saw it in New York. Great exhibit."

"And the monument you're working on will be great too, Patty." Claire smiled at her.

Patty beamed. "Well, I hope you all say that when you come to the grand opening of the monument next year."

Fanny smiled. "I'm sure we will."

"Hey, guess what Martina said last week?" Jo-Jo sat up.

"What?" asked Noreen.

"Well," Jo-Jo continued, "I just read about this in *Newsweek*. Apparently a reporter asked her: 'Ms Navratilova, are you still a lesbian?' She looked at him and responded: 'Are you still the alternative?'"

They roared with laughter.

"Great march last week, wasn't it?" Patty asked. "At least, I had a great time. You did too, didn't you Claire?"

"Yes, I did. Very well organized."

"I think we were all pretty brave to go last year and it paid off. Everyone who came the past two years was brave to do so," Denise said, always being the therapist. "Numbers were up from last year, everything was peaceful, and the March was back to being what it used to be."

"It sure seemed a lot better without those bozos there, didn't it?" Noreen piped in.

Merle looked at Fanny and they raised their glasses.

"Here's to the women," Fanny toasted.

"To women," the seven women all echoed, glasses raised.

Jo-Jo leaned back against the dark orange sofa. She felt so pleased with her decision to stay in Calgary and especially pleased with her new friends. They had all grown so much closer over the year. She knew she made the right decision to live in Calgary. Her mother, Marcy, was recovering well from her chemotherapy and she spoke with her daily and saw her almost as often. Her job was going extremely well, and her last assessment was better than she could have ever hoped. And with all that, she still managed to get out to the mountains several times a month. Lately on occasion, Marcy had gone with her.

THEY WERE SEATED around the table, ready to begin the second course of the gourmet meal—rack of lamb surrounding a mound of wild rice with mushrooms.

"Hey, guess who I had coffee with last week?" Noreen asked.

"I'll bite," said Patty, "who?"

"Joanie and Angie. Angie is doing really well after the accident. You know, she was in hospital about three months. But now she's back at work."

"That's great," Jo-Jo said.

"Yeah, it is," Noreen continued. "And the two of them are both in a new lab and just loving the work. Joanie seems as if a huge weight has been lifted off her shoulders."

"Well, it has," said Claire, "and his name was Sonderman."
Everyone laughed.

"It seemed as though the army was taking forever to get him, didn't it?" Patty asked.

"Yes, but at least he is now in prison where he belongs," Merle said. "Although I heard through the grapevine that his lawyers were trying to get him transferred to a psychiatric hospital."

"Jail, nut house, who cares. As long as he's locked up and can't hurt anyone anymore," Patty said. "He sure was a mean son of a bitch."

"That he was, that he was," Fanny replied.

"And while we're on the topic," Jo-Jo put her fork down on the salad plate, "what's Clovis up to these days? Has he finished his community service?"

"Oh, he's down on the first floor, cleaning up the undergraduate lab, doing the mediocre work he does so well." Noreen laughed along with the others.

"I guess it's a good thing he's unable to read people's emotions," Denise offered.

"That makes it a lot easier for him to work at cleaning labs. He has no idea what people are thinking. At least he's back at the university where he wanted to be, even if in a slightly different capacity." Patty laughed.

"In a way," Claire added, "it's kind of sad he didn't get his job back. I really think he was badly used by that General. Poor Clovis."

"Poor Clovis, indeed," said Patty. "He has to be responsible for his own actions."

"Yes, he does," agreed Claire, "and he will be paying for his poor judgement for the rest of his life." She sighed sadly.

"Here's a bit of news," Noreen said. "I just heard this in the Science Building a few weeks ago. I guess Clovis had been approached by some journalist who wanted to do a big article about what happened with him last year. I heard that now they might be writing a book. So who knows. Maybe he will be famous after all."
They all chuckled.

"And you know," Claire put her fork down exactly in the centre of her plate, "they finally decided what to do with those viruses. They actually destroyed them, just last month. The army finally allowed that they were done with them and didn't need them anymore. As if they ever needed them. At any rate, according to the army, in conjunction with the head of the Science Department, the viruses Clovis discovered no longer exist in this world. Just as well."

"Whatever happened to that lovely wig?" Jo-Jo asked.

They erupted with laughter.

"I think I can safely say," Jo-Jo tried to stop laughing, "that my life has not been the same since that first night we broke into the old lab on the third floor. In fact, y'know that art thing you have hanging by your front door?"

"Which one?" Denise asked.

"The one by Ntozake Shange, you know, the one with the beautiful colours that says 'Where there is a Woman, There is Magic.' I thought it was wonderful when I first saw it years ago, but I didn't realize at the time that you all live it. It has been magic, these past few years. Thank you, all of you, for taking me in."

"Aw, Jo-Jo, that's so sweet," Patty teased, half-seriously.

"I mean it," Jo-Jo got serious. "I will always look for the magic from now on, whenever I am in the presence of women."

Denise looked around the table. "And I'm sure you'll find it, Jo-Jo. We all will."

Ruth Simkin's published books include *What Makes You Happy*, a book of short stories, *The Jagged Years of Ruthie J*, a memoir which met with critical acclaim, and *Like an Orange on a Seder Plate, a Lesbian Haggadah*. She has written countless medical papers and contributed to textbooks, as well as doing many mixed media presentations. She has published many non-medical articles and booklets on a variety of topics. She currently lives with her Golden Doodle, Kelly, and when she is not writing, is contentedly reflecting on the ocean, the flora and the wildlife around her home.

Made in the USA
Columbia, SC
12 March 2018